The Witching Hour

Thrillers, Chillers, Mysteries and Twists

Sarah England

Copyright © 2013 by Sarah England
Artwork: RoseWolf Design
All rights reserved.

No part of this book may be used or reproduced in any manner whatsoever without written permission of the author, except for brief quotations used for promotion or in reviews. This is a work of fiction. Names, characters, places, and incidents are used fictitiously. Any resemblance to actual persons living or dead, business establishments, events, or locales, is entirely coincidental.

All of the stories in this collection have been previously published in national magazines or anthologies.

ISBN: 9781543134636

About the author: Sarah England originally trained as a nurse in Sheffield (UK), before working in the pharmaceutical industry and specialising in mental health – a theme which creeps into many of her stories. To date she has had over 160 short stories and serials published in magazines and newspapers before having her first novel published in 2013.

At the fore of Sarah's body of work is the bestselling trilogy of occult horror novels – Father of Lies, Tanners Dell and Magda; shortly to be followed by The Owlmen – due out on April 26th, 2018.

You might also enjoy, The Soprano – A Haunting Supernatural Thriller set on the North Staffordshire Moors.

If you would like to be informed about future releases, there is a newsletter sign-up on Sarah's website, the details of which follow here. Please feel free to keep in touch via any of the social media channels, too. It's good to hear from you!

http://www.sarahenglandauthor.co.uk

Books by S. E. England

Father of Lies – An Occult Horror Trilogy, Book 1
Tanners Dell - Book 2
Magda – Book 3
The Soprano – A Supernatural Thriller
The Owlmen – Pure Occult Horror - out 26th April, 2018

Contents

1. Out of the Woods
2. Someone Out There: Part 1 - 3
3. Rough Love
4. Cold Melon Tart
5. The Witching Hour
6. Girl in the Rain
7. The Last Bus Home
8. The Midnight People
9. 'Buried Too Deep': Parts 1 - 3
10. Headache
11. A Second Opinion
12. Retribution
13. Moving In
14. Masquerade
15. Adele
16. Night Duty
17. Rosie and Joe
18. Sixty Seconds
19. House Hunt
20. The Witchfinders

1. Out of the Woods

Jack felt himself being watched as he locked the church door. Turning, he squinted into the low, winter sun and noticed a familiar figure leaning against one of the gravestones. Although eighteen years had passed since he had last seen him, Toby had never really gone away - haunting his thoughts and possessing his nightmares as if everything had happened only yesterday.

Their eyes locked and darkness rushed in like heat from an oven…*Tangled branches, blinding panic, pounding feet. Solid black, couldn't see, stumbling, on his knees, up again, running and running…*

"Tobes," he said, with a forced smile. "Long time no see. How're things?" Toby's dark eyes searched his own, touching a deep secret and painfully wrenching it free.

"It's time, Jack," said Toby, quietly. "This thing isn't going to go away."

He tried to steady the jackhammer of his heart, his voice barely above a whisper. "What is it? What's happened?"

"It's Leo. My son. He's acting weird, saying things… Jack, I know it sounds impossible but - he knows. He knows everything."

"What do you mean? He can't do."

"We need to talk." Toby indicated his car.

The wind was whipping up, granite clouds scudding fast and low. Jack dipped his head as he plodded after Toby. Nothing good was going to come of today.

Moments later they were sitting in Toby's comfortably upholstered Volvo Estate, baby-seat in the back, tissues and half eaten bags of sweets evidence of a normal family life.

Jack pressed his fingers to his temples. Eighteen years and not a word of contact. Eighteen years of professionalism, of prayer and atonement - of waking in the small hours soaked in sweat, the subconscious surfacing nightly to remind him of what happened. And now this. Of course...of course, they would have to pay... How could they go forward as respectable professionals - he a priest, Toby a doctor – safe and rewarded after what they'd done?

Toby sighed heavily. The last time the two of them had spoken it had been in similar circumstances. As teenagers in Toby's white van - sitting on scuffed, torn seats with bits of foam spilling out - Jack staring straight ahead, Toby slumped over the steering wheel. The smell of sweat and fear hung heavily in the air after spending most of the weekend in the police station.

"You didn't tell them anything, did you?" Toby had said.

"Of course I bloody didn't."

Later, they would go home and shower until their skins burned, scrubbing and scrubbing as if it was possible to cleanse their souls into shiny new things again instead of what they now were - dirty, rotten, debased.

The interrogation had been relentless for

both boys, going round and round in circles with neither of them saying anything other than they couldn't remember. It was supposed to have been a laugh. A camping trip. But when they woke up, Marilyn, Jack's sister, had vanished.

After that they had tacitly agreed to keep a distance, get on with life, try to forget...Until today.

Toby cleared his throat. "It's Leo, he's–"

A strong gust rattled the car and a shower of golden leaves scattered across the bonnet. Jack's stomach tightened. The afternoon was darkening already, unnaturally so. "Go on."

"God knows I've tried to do the right things in life–" Toby raked his hair into a rooster look. "Worked so damn hard, looked after my patients, my family...But it's not going to go away, Jack. It's started up again."

"What's happening with Leo?" Jack prompted.

"Yeah, my eldest. Fine...I mean he was absolutely fine - bright, healthy, sociable. Then he turned thirteen and well, Eve noticed it first - things being moved around in his room when he wasn't there. She'd put a pile of towels down on his bed and when she came back they'd be in the middle of the floor - things like that. Odd noises in the night - his computer flashing up, TV switching itself on while he was fast asleep...And then one morning he told me something calmly as you like...He said, 'Dad, I know what you've done, you know?' And then he laughed. I mean – the kid's eyes were sparkling. I asked him, jokingly, if he meant the beer stash I'd got in for the match at the weekend without Mum knowing. I had my back to him getting some milk out of the fridge…But when I turned round his expression knocked the breath out of me. He said, 'I mean – I know where Marilyn is. I know what you did.'

"But you'd never told him. Never told anyone, right? Not even Eve?"

"Of course bloody not. Are you mad?" He raked his hair again and again until it resembled a cockatoo. Then turned and looked directly at Jack, steady and serious, his eyes red-rimmed and pained. "Jack, I'm not messing around. I think he's possessed. By Marilyn's spirit–"

"What?"

"It's her inside of him – the stuff he knows–"

Jack quelled a surge of nausea as he tried to make sense of the information. Marilyn was his sister. And the way she died had been horrifically disturbing.

"Why? I mean, what the hell makes you think that?"

"It's okay – I expected you to be angry and I didn't expect you to believe me. But you are the only one who can understand and the only one who can help. If this comes out–"

"Yes, yes…Just tell me!"

"Jack, he speaks with her voice. Only to me. It's at night – he wakes shouting – crying out like he's having a nightmare. I'll rush to his room and that's when he changes in the flick of a light switch, from a terrified boy to this – well, to this malicious girl. And it's her: she does that thing with her hair - you know, flicking it back? And bats her eyelashes at me with those sly eyes – from my son's face! And then out comes this low, seductive voice."

"Saying what?"

"Saying she's watching us both and the truth will out."

"Hang on - you're seriously telling me that my dead sister is speaking through Leo?"

"Yes, that's what I am seriously telling you. And I'm also seriously telling you that it's true because he told me exactly where Marilyn was and he's right."   Jack opened the car door and hurried onto the grass where he quietly vomited, then stood panting and sweating, propped against a gravestone with one hand while Toby waited and watched from the car. Maybe Toby was mad, the guilt finally getting to him? These were his friend's own demons…Yet something told him no, after what he had witnessed all those years ago, this was possible. And worse, there was more to come. He quickly recited a short prayer. He would need all his strength because, dear God, Toby wanted something from him. And he knew for sure what it would be.

***

His sister, Marilyn, had always been trouble, and never in a million light years should they have let her persuade them to go on that trip.

It was Toby's fault – him and his bloody hormones.

"Come on you pair of lightweights. It's just a laugh. A teeny-weeny little séance in the woods. We can tell the parents it's just a camping trip. Cathy's up for it, Jack!"

Back then, he'd had a thing for Cathy with her baby-blonde hair and wide blue eyes - a girl who did whatever Marilyn told her – and for a moment he'd wavered. Then baulked at the obvious manipulation and changed his mind back again.

"No freaking way."

"Come on - I've got the Ouija Board," Marilyn said, green eyes dancing with excitement. "It'll be such a laugh." And then she played her Ace. Sidling up to Toby she whispered in his ear, and seconds later Toby was grinning like an oaf.

His sister had long, black hair, a body she knew how to flaunt and wickedly upturned lips. She liked to watch the effect she had on boys…husbands…fathers…

Even when Cathy dropped out at the last minute on some pathetic excuse he couldn't even recall, Toby was still keen, so whatever she'd said had him hooked for sure. "Come on mate, it's just a camping trip. Let her do her spooky stuff if she wants. I've got some cans and some E's."

So he'd gone with them. A gooseberry in petulant mood.

They'd set up camp at the far end of the woods near to where the new bypass was being built, the night the blackest he could ever remember - no moon, no stars, and no wind to hurry along the thick, grey clouds that hung wet and low. Late autumn, the air was smoky and cold already, the leaves on the forest floor dead and soggy. He and Toby lit a small fire, while Marilyn drew a circle in the dirt, positioned the candles and instructed them to sit round the Ouija board.

For a while, as they gulped vodka, there were just each other's faces, bobbing eerily in the candlelight, alive with anticipation, excitement, and a tinge of fear in the deathly hush of the woods.

***

To this day, Jack could still envisage Marilyn's sly grin and taunting eyes, her hair hanging long and loose as she stared at his friend with openly sexual intent. He took a tissue from his coat pocket, dabbed at his face, then slowly walked back to the car. She had been messing around with the occult for months, and who knew what dark spirits had been invited in? If only he'd known back then what he knew now. Opening the passenger door he sat next to Toby and said, "Okay, so what are we going to do, then?"

"Eve wants him to go to a psychiatrist, but then of course she would, she doesn't know the history. He's not ill, though, Jack. This is your department. You're a priest. We can't let him start talking - bringing it up. Someone might investigate. Honestly, I don't think we even have a choice here. You have to exorcise him."

He knew this was coming. Yet still his stomach flipped and sweat beaded across his forehead. "I've never done one."

"But you could, couldn't you? Jack, we can't let him talk. He's getting more and more insistent. He was very precise."

Jack said nothing, busy thinking about how the Church would baulk at this, how he wasn't qualified and would never get permission. Not that he could present the truth…

"I thought we were out of the woods," Toby was saying. "God, I've spent most of my life never doing anything wrong ever again - I don't drop so much as a sweet wrapper."

Jack nodded. How he had prayed and prayed for forgiveness.

"And what good would it do for us to go to prison now? We're valuable, respectable professionals. People need us, look up to us. What good would it do?"   Jack nodded again.

"And Leo needs help. He's getting worse – unsociable, rude, isolated and changeable. I'm afraid for him."

"Yes."

Toby stared at his profile. "So you will–?"

"Damn Marilyn!"

Suddenly the car shook, rocking in a particularly violent blast of wind, leaves swirling around the windows.

"Let's do it, then," said Toby.

***

"It's called 'Listen to the Glass'," Marilyn explained.

The three of them put their hand on the upturned wineglass.

Nothing happened. But just as Jack was shaking his head and Toby started to fidget, the wineglass shot round the Ouija board.

"Stop it, Marilyn! You're making it move."

"Keep your hands on the glass. It's not me–"

Behind them the forest stilled to an eerie silence. Not a single leaf rustled. No owls hooted and not a creature stirred in the undergrowth. It was as if life itself dared not breathe. The fire flared wildly without a skein of wind, and the candles burned ever brighter.

Marilyn's laugh rang loud and shrill.

"Whoa! Tripping like freak here!" said Toby, washing down an E.

Marilyn took the vodka bottle and poured more down her throat, letting it spill onto her top so Toby could see she had nothing on underneath. "Is there a spirit with us?" she asked in a mocking voice.

The glass shot to YES.

"Who?"

M A R I L Y N

Then without any warning a hiking boot flew across the board, slamming into the trees behind.

"Holy shit," said Jack, leaping to his feet.

Marilyn seemed thrilled. "It works, it

works!" Tipping more vodka down her throat, she wiped her full, blood red mouth with the back of her hand and grinned.

"Do you mean us harm?" she asked, with a giggle.

The boys, both now standing and ready to run, looked at each other, ashen faced. "Let's stop now, Marilyn."

This time the glass flew round on its own, without any hands on it. YES

Marilyn sat back, watching the words being spelled out in quick succession right before their eyes: B I T C H G E T O U T L E A V E.

By then it was hard to breathe properly, the air close, soupy and heavy, laced with a cloying scent reminiscent of rotting flowers, filling their lungs and dragging at their limbs. Everything seemed to be in slow motion. The smoke thickened and a storm whistled in the trees, causing the flames to fly from the fire. Then suddenly the board flew into the air and this was where events blurred in Jack's mind. Marilyn had jumped up, swathed in flames, her hair and clothing on fire, screaming…

***

In the two days before the trip with Toby and Leo, Jack did his best to prepare. It would test his faith to the limit and the Church would have no knowledge of this: details would be required and neither he nor Toby could risk the truth being exposed. Hopefully, whatever was taking a hold of

Leo would be exorcised right here and right now, and then they could get on with their lives.

He crossed himself, holding the bible in his anorak pocket, as the three of them headed into the woods with rucksacks and provisions for a weekend of fishing and games.

This time the night was lit by a waning moon and a hazy galaxy of stars. Their breath steamed in the cold air as they tramped deeper and deeper towards the centre of the forest. They could not, Jack told them gravely, afford to be discovered.

"Not where we were before though, eh?" said Toby, constantly checking over his shoulder.

"No."

But once amongst the trees their bearings became muddled and it wasn't long before the roar of the bypass could be heard in the distance.

"We've come too far," said Toby. "Let's backtrack a bit."

"You've been here before, haven't you?" said Leo. "Right here – in this exact spot?"

Open mouthed, both men turned to look at him. Both denied it. Leo shrugged but he kept looking at his father with darkening eyes that glinted with a knowledge older than his years.

Toby rubbed his hands together, pretending a paternal confidence and jollity he didn't feel. "Right, okay then. Let's go further back, nearer the stream and then set up camp before it gets too dark, eh?"

Running as fast as a hunted fox, clawing at

dry twigs snapping in the face, gripping onto the weight in the sheet that slipped and slithered, fingers of darkness clutching at their clothes, nearly there, panting, limbs screaming, lungs bursting... After supper, with the fire crackling nicely, Jack suggested a game of cards. If he tried hard enough he could almost make himself believe this really was a camping trip with an old mate and his boy. But there was a weight pressing in, an omnipotent, whispering presence, making his head pound and his heart race. He glanced over his shoulder. Night had descended like the blackest curtain, chasing away all vestiges of daylight and bringing with it an ancient, primeval fear of the dark - of things unknown and powers unseen, which, as he well knew, could bring madness and destroy souls.

The lit candle of faith deep within him flickered and faltered. This would be his ultimate test and he could almost hear Marilyn laughing.

"Coffee?" suggested Toby.

"Please." Jack took a grateful sip. He must help Leo. Help them all. He must not, could not, fail. "Leo, you know I'm a priest?"

Leo nodded.

"Your dad says you've been feeling a bit disturbed recently about some of the things that have happened, and I'd like to say a little prayer – see if we can get rid of whatever it is troubling you. Would that be okay?"

Leo nodded. "Sure! Is that why you got me here? To stop all the weird stuff going on?"

Jack smiled. "Partly. And we wanted an

excuse for a camping trip, of course - away from the girls and all that." Flashing into his mind came the distorted, anguished face of his mother eighteen years ago, together with the aching, empty feeling that had dogged the rest of his years.

The only sound now came from the nearby stream - trickling over rocks and pebbles - hypnotic, soothing, cold and real.

Tony and Leo were watching him. Waiting.

Jack blessed the holy water he'd brought with him and was about to begin the prayer when Leo said in Marilyn's low, husky voice, "What did you do with the board, Jack?"

He jolted visibly. "Pardon?"

"The Ouija board," said Leo, batting his eyelashes. "What did you do with it? Because if you burnt it then the evil spirit you raised will stay around forever. You'll never get rid of it no matter what you do."

***

It had taken what seemed like hours but somehow Jack and Toby had managed to put out the blaze. Marilyn had burst into an immediate and ferocious inferno. Within seconds the fireball was white-hot and even though they had frantically grabbed groundsheets to throw over her, it was too late. They rolled her body back and forth in the damp, autumn leaves until there was nothing left but a blackened corpse and the acrid smell of burning flesh.

They'd stood gasping for breath, choking from the smoke; red, stinging eyes staring with horror at the sight before them. Jack sank to his knees, pushing his fist into his mouth to stop himself from screaming.

The wind had dropped, and once more the woods were still and silent. "We have to bury her," said Toby. "Quick, think, think. Nobody in the world will believe us. No one. Did you see it? Did you see the flames go crazy like that?" Jack had been too numb to speak, too petrified to move. Nobody would believe them, he'd got that right.

The night had been still. The wind had whipped up from nowhere. Yet she'd been caught in a fireball - in some kind of freak tornado.

Toby was right. He was right… And his sister was dead. In the end he'd let himself be told what to do, had done what Toby said and rolled Marilyn's body, which was little more than a bundle of blackened bones and dripping sinews, back into the sheet. And then they'd run like wild animals from guns, racing over rocks and streams, tripping over gnarled roots, falling into ditches, branches scratching at their eyes… The new bypass was near, the site deserted and the foundations for the bridge deep.

"Drop her down there and the new bridge will go on top," said Toby. "Come on, Jack, we have to do it. We have to."

Then emerging from the woods in the early hours, they'd told the world that they had woken up to find that Marilyn had gone. Vanished.

***

On the day following the camping trip, Toby's wife, Eve, arrived home to find a police officer waiting for her. Bundling the younger children inside, she hurried over to the patrol car. "Oh my God, what's happened? Is it Leo?"

Quickly she took in the information as the officer began to explain. And as he spoke, the sooty, tired looking face of her eldest son peered at her from the back seat. Found, the police officer was saying, stumbling along the roadside near to a local beauty spot - a wooded area on the edge of town.

"So what happened? Where are Toby and his friend, Jack?"

The police officer inclined his head towards the house. "I think perhaps we should go indoors. The boy says they disappeared. He woke up and they'd gone. Vanished."

"What?"

"We have to take him in for questioning, obviously. In the meantime, may I ask if you and your husband were having difficulties? If perhaps there was somewhere he was planning on going? A relative, a friend–?"

Eve, wild-eyed and distracted, shook her head. "No."

She looked over his shoulder to Leo in the car. "Leo?"

Calmly he eyed her back. Flicked his hair and, very faintly, smiled.

THE END

Out of The Woods was first published by: 1. Scream: anthology by Bridge House Publishing in 2010, ISBN: 978-1-907335-00-6.
2. Ether books.com 2011

2. Someone Out There: Part 1 - 3

Part 1

January 1983

Five year old Alice traced patterns through the condensation with her small, chubby fingers. A fresh flurry of sleety snow spattered the windowpane, and a raw Northerly buffeted the house and rattled the chimney pot.

Inside the sparsely furnished front room, sooty smoke clogged the air, and damp washing steamed in front of the fire. Through the wall to the scullery came the shrill sound of her mother shouting. Occasionally there was a loud bang as if someone had hit the table with a fist, her father's angry roar rising over the top of her mother's shrieking tirade.

Sucking her thumb, Alice looked outside - at shivering blades of grass now coated in silvery white; at the towering moors beyond. The afternoon was closing in, silent, steady, grey.

Cold fingers. She hugged her hands tightly inside her cardigan. Cold toes too - clenched over and over inside cotton socks.

It wasn't her fault. None of this was her fault. She'd been hungry.

"Well, we're all hungry," her mother had snapped. The sting of her mother's slap still burned the back of her legs, along with the fresh memory of red-faced fury, fingers digging into her shoulders. "Your dad on the dole and me having to work like a slave just to put food on the table; and here you are helping yourself. Do you think I enjoy taking washing in? Do you?"

"But it wasn't me," she wailed.

"Well if it wasn't you it must have been the fairies again then?" her mother said, shaking her head in disgust. "No one likes a liar, Alice."

But it wasn't her, it really wasn't. The brightly wrapped chocolates in the shiny tin had been too much of a temptation for Baby Alice - the other girl - the one with the rumbling tummy, who did all the bad things. Like eating chocolates and then scrunching up the foils again to make it look like she hadn't.

"I was saving those for when we have visitors. Still - it'd be that mysterious fairy friend of yours again, I expect," said her mother, before slamming the door behind her to 'make a start on tea'. "The one who's so convenient whenever there's any trouble around?"

It was why they were rowing anyway, Alice knew. All she could hear was, 'that girl this, and that girl that.' The voices rising. Gaining momentum along with the beat of her heart. Suddenly there came the sound of a door being kicked - so hard it shook the walls and jack-hammered her heart... Burning vegetables. A cold draught. Alice began to hum. Tracing snowflakes. Humming. That naughty girl. Not herself. She was the good one.

Later, she couldn't say how long - minutes, hours - the fire cracked and a spark flew across the red, nylon carpet. Alice jumped awake. The light had changed. And a black hole smoked where the ember had landed. Finding herself alone and stiff limbed, curled in a tight ball behind the sofa underneath the window sill - her favourite hiding place - silence echoed in the lengthening shadows of the room. The day had faded to a soft, ethereal whiteness - swirling eddies of snow settling steadily in a deathly blanket. The house darkening, chilling by degrees.

Pulling herself up, she looked up at the ominously rolling clouds. The family car was being pushed out of the driveway, her mother, grim-faced, at the wheel, her father holding a spade in one hand as he leaned his weight against the boot.

They were leaving. Slipping away like thieves. And who could blame them for abandoning the bad girl. Alice banged her fists on the window. Tears rolled down her cheeks. She'd be good from now on. She was the good one… if only they believed her.

***

Friday - last day of the week, thank goodness. Beth slung her sopping gym bag over her shoulder and jumped off the school bus. Now for the trek over the moor - grand on a summer day but torture in weather like this. All afternoon on the freezing hockey fields with her legs stung raw with sleet, her face numb and hair dripping down her back. And if that wasn't enough, she was starting with a cold.

Slipping and sliding, she dipped her head against the oncoming blizzard and tried to ignore the screaming chilblains in her sodden shoes. Just think of the nice, warm fire, she promised herself as she tramped higher and higher, and a hot cup of tea. She'd soon be home. Oh how she envied her schoolmates in town - it was only sleeting there, just wet and cold. While up here it was a white-out already.

Why was she the one who had to live miles out of town in a near-deserted mining village? Bad enough she couldn't go to the pictures with Richie tomorrow night. Oh to think of them all going out without her….It just wasn't fair. Richie with his floppy fair hair and sparkling hazel eyes. He only had to look at her to make her stomach flip. He'd even bought her Duran Duran's latest single, and now whenever she heard, *'her name was Rio and she danced upon the sand'*... she'd see him. Always.

God how she wanted to escape! Counting the days now….she was almost fifteen. Squinting into the fast-fading light, she could just make out the skeletal outline of the pit head, the wheel axle silhouetted against a bruised sky. At the sight of it Beth's stomach clenched as it never failed to do - something about the haunting cries of miners trapped in underground accidents, their moans sighing through the tunnels. Her own late father's and grandad's….She pulled up her scarf to shield her face from the biting wind and scanned the skyline. Spectres flurried in the swirls of snow, icy fingers pulling her towards the shaft.....sooty hands reaching out of the ground to grab at her ankles....too many horror stories....Beth pushed them from her mind, but picked up pace.

In the distance the row of three terraces in which she lived, was vaguely visible - huddled together in a ghostly apparition of blackened stone and coiling smoke plumes. No strings of washing blowing flat out in the wind today. Auntie Nell's place would be steaming with wet washing, awaiting the small spin-dryer in the scullery - sheets and underwear strewn across the kitchen, shirts lumped over clothes-horses in the front room, towels dripping over the bath. Nell would be in a temper and she was glad her own mother, Margaret, was a gentler soul. Maybe they'd have little Alice over for tea if things were difficult next door again.

She and Adam would play board games with her and try to make her smile. He was old and boring, of course, and not at all good looking with those NHS specs and goofy teeth. Bit of hissed gossip about Violet and how she came to have a son so long after the two girls were born. Not gossip she understood or cared about though. That was then. History. Old people.

Things had got worse for them when the pit closed, though. Only Uncle Harry, Auntie Nell's husband, still worked there. Because he'd had polio as a child, he'd been in the office, and his income had kept Nell and Alice, with enough left over to help Nell's mother Violet and her son, Adam. Now they had nothing. Harry spent his days looking through the local paper for work that never came, and Nell took in washing. The three terraces. Three broken families. Beth shivered.

Trudging on, concentrating now, Beth climbed methodically, breath tight in her lungs. Almost at the pit head and then it would be downhill all the way. At the top she paused for a minute, bent double, holding her knees, aware of an eerie silence. A lull.

Suddenly the wind howled like an express train, flattening skeletal trees and shards of grass. Freezing sleet slashed into her face. The snow clutched at her feet as they sank into iciness. She gasped. Then blinked. What the heck was that?

There was someone out here!

Coming out of the blizzard.

She stood for a moment, locked in indecision. Staring hard. No, it couldn't be. But there was no mistake. Lurching towards her out of the gloom came the lumbering figure of a man calling out her name.

And then she ran, tearing down the hill in panic stricken leaps. A ghost from the mine. A ghost holding out its hands to strangle her with.

***

March 2013

D.I. Phil Blackmore was waiting for her when she arrived at the station, fingers tapping a file, itching to get to work on something. Spying him through the small window in the door, Beth ducked into the changing rooms and took her time.

Let him wake up with the mother of all headaches after yet another night of sleeplessness, and see if he still feels as sprightly as a mountain goat! Oh dear - peep hole red eyes and great carrier bags underneath - why oh why was insomnia kicking in now, at this time of life? She was secure in her job, and content in her two-bed flat by the river. Mum had been gone now for over three years and even Alice, her cousin, was finally settled after all the past turmoil. So why now?

Sighing, Beth applied mascara and lipstick, tied back her hair and washed her hands. Oh well, another day, another case…hopefully something she could get her teeth into.

Phil smiled as she walked in; looked pointedly at his watch. "Hope we're not keeping you awake, D.C. Porter?"

Beth smiled back. Oh let him have his little flirt. Why not? It was fun and it made their sometimes grim tasks, a whole lot easier. In another life she might even find him attractive. If he wasn't so freshly divorced and if he wasn't her boss and if….well if she wanted a man in her life… that was all. Which she definitely didn't.

She took the carton of coffee he offered and took a grateful sip.

"Only here's something here you're going to be interested in." He tapped the bulging file. "Body's been found down a mine shaft. Well, I say body - skeletal remains would be more accurate, thirty years or so… "

" …well there were a lot of mining

accidents and not all the bodies were found, you know?"

Phil narrowed his eyes. "Ah there's no getting past you D.C. Porter. Thing is - this one had its skull caved in at the back - a blunt injury and quite a big one. And it was directly at the bottom of the shaft - give or take a few scattered bones - not something a search team would have missed."

...oh, and if he wasn't so irritating...

"It be murder then," Beth said in her most dramatic impersonation of a hammy actor.

"Aye it be. And in your home village too."

The mood changed in an instant. She put down her coffee.

"What do you mean? *My home village?*"

"You lived out at Rock Edge when you were growing up, didn't you? The back of beyond, miles from anywhere? Complete with ghosts and white-outs every winter?"

"The body was there? At Rock Edge? At the pit?"

"Yes. Why?"

She shook her head, as if trying to clear it. Her father and grandfather were dead and buried. And Uncle Harry and Auntie Nell were long gone - to Scarborough, according to her mother, who'd kept in touch until she died three years ago. And Adam had just been a boy - a few years older than herself - he'd gone to college and now ran a landscape gardening business in Leeds.

"It's got to be someone from out of the area. There were - are - only our three terraces, and no one was reported missing from down in the village or my mother would have known, and Gran certainly would: nothing got past Violet. No, someone dumped this body down a disused mine and did not expect it to be found."

"Which it wouldn't have been if a bloke hadn't been letting his Jack Russell chase rabbits up on the moors. The dog fell down the shaft and that's when the rescue team found more than they bargained for."

"Do we have an identity yet?"

Phil shook his head. "Forensics are on it. Meanwhile we have to do a bit of good old fashioned detective work - question the folk at Rock Edge and see if anyone can remember a darned thing from about thirty years ago."

"You're sure it's thirty years?"

"Apparently, that's not the difficult bit. Thirty years is pretty definite as is the fact that it's young and male. You would have known him, surely?"

"Well no."

"One of your lot must have seen something. You said your house overlooked the pit. And all that gossip - must've been rife with 'nowt else to do on yet another miserable night on t' moors.'"

"All right - Mr Sophisticated of Pontefract...Yes, our houses are close to the pit - we can see the pit head from our bedroom windows - but whoever tipped a body down there would have done it at night, Detective Inspector Blackmore. Surely?"

He nodded. "Tyre tracks, D.C. Porter? 'Nothing gets past your grandmother, Violet, D.C. Porter?'"

"Apart from that."

"Right. Missing persons check. Forensics. Questioning the locals." He looked at his watch again. "You and me - how about it?"

"Pardon?"

"After we've finished work how about a pie and a pint? What did you think I meant?"

Beth smiled. "Exactly that. But you'll have to go to Rock Edge without me - I've got to finish a report from yesterday and it's my day to go and see Alice."

No way, in fact, was she going to go to Rock Edge ever again, either with or without him. She'd left at sixteen and never looked back. This murder had nothing to do with her personally and she didn't need to go. Ever. No way. End of.

His twinkly blue eyes stopped twinkling as they bore into hers. "But of course! We can start interviewing the locals right here and now, can we not? My office, Beth - as of five minutes ago."

***

Oh why, why, why? Thirty years ago she'd left the God-forsaken place and vowed never to return. Even when Mum died: the funeral had been at the church in the neighbouring village where she'd been laid to rest next to Beth's father, Roy. There had been few possessions and she'd told Violet to take what she liked.

Phil fetched fresh coffees and sat behind

his desk, watching her. "I don't get it, Beth. What's so bad about the place? Just that it's haunted with old wives' tales? What?"

"Dad used to say they'd be working hard when they'd all hear it at once - the sound of moaning - trapped miners from years before. Men never found. Buried in rubble...And then he and Grandad both...Well, you can hear it when you're walking up there." Beth shuddered.

"Okay, I can understand that. You didn't like living up there and it was spooky."

"Bad memories, Phil. I lost most of my family up there."

"Yes. I know. But this is a murder case. Someone dumped this body within yards of where you lived at the time you lived there. One of you must have seen or heard something. You would have been what - fifteen? Sixteen?"

"I was busy at fifteen/sixteen." She almost smiled, remembering just how busy she'd actually been with her gaggle of under-age, drunken friends as they lurched along on pub crawls, hoping to see the boys from school. Spiky haired boys in clompy boots; New Order pumping out from under doorways...*Boy was she busy...*

"Trouble with obsessive people like you and me - we're never in the moment are we? Too busy thinking about other things, missing facts staring at us in the here and now. .You were busy thinking about lads and planning your escape. But you may still have seen or heard something relevant. You know that. I know that. Which is why I need you to think hard about anything unusual you may have encountered around that time."

She shook her head. "Nope. Nothing."

"What about a car showing up you hadn't seen before? Any gossip you overheard you couldn't make sense of?"

"No."

"Surnames - Violet and Adam…?"

"May."

"Nell and is it Harry?"

"Birch."

He stared at her for a few more minutes. Unblinking. Heat crept into her face. There *was* something. Something that blew like tumbleweed through the corridors of her mind, something haunting her dreams…being chased by the ghost on the moors…Someone in the background, on the edge…..Oh but she couldn't tell him vague things like that. It sounded silly even to herself. "No," she repeated. "There was nothing."

***

Driving over to Alice's small semi later that afternoon, the day darkened in an instant. One moment Beth was driving and the next she'd screeched the car into a lay-by.   Breathing hard. Sweat poured down her back. Her heart thumped heavily in her chest. The car was too small. She had to get out.

Breathe…breathe…rationalise this - it must be a panic attack…just breathe…

A few minutes later she found herself gripping the steering wheel, knuckles white, but seeing clearly. It was over. A cyclist knocked on her window and she buzzed it down. "You all right?"

She nodded. "Thanks."

Two things, her brain computed, first of all the nightmares were getting worse, and secondly this murder had something to do with her. 'Think,' Phil had said, and she deliberately hadn't. Why? It was as if, she thought, starting up the car again, her memories wanted out. Memories she didn't want to have. Memories locked up, so dark she couldn't admit to having them at all, let alone discuss them with anyone else.

No way could she face Alice today either. Dear, fragile Alice with her pills, anxiety problems and therapy sessions. Much as she loved her cousin, being with Alice took a lot of energy and today she didn't have any. Today she could happily sleep on the tarmac while shoppers trampled over her body, she was that tired.

In fact what she'd do instead, was go straight home and go to bed with a hot water bottle. She was coming down with something - a twenty-four hour thing probably. Phil would have to go to Rock Edge without her tomorrow. She couldn't question her own grandmother about police matters anyway. Ridiculous. Totally. Although she didn't want D.C. Marie Bell going over there either, delving into her past and seeing where she used to live. Oh the horror. ...Anyway, she still couldn't go. It was probably linked to some gangland murder or something. Nothing to do with herself. She could go to bed, wake up and it would all be over.

The call came while she was putting the kettle on.

Beth glanced at the little screen. Forensics. "D.C. Porter?"

"Speaking."

"We've got an identity on the body in the mine shaft. "

A chill whispered through her veins. The floor swayed. Something coming - a premonition....Beth gripped the work top. "Go on."

"We've got a match on dental records. It's Adam May. Early twenties. I understand from D.I. Blackmore that you knew him? That you are related to his mother?"

The walls closed in on her. She sank to the floor. "No. No, it isn't him. Adam's alive. He runs a landscape gardening business in Leeds. I get Christmas cards…"

There came a deep intake of breath from across the airwaves. "There's no doubt, I'm afraid, D.C. Porter. It's definitely him."

***

Part 2

At 7 a.m. the March mist lay thickly over the moors - an impenetrable bank of gloom, drizzling miserably over endless miles of sodden turf.

D.I. Phil Blackmore pulled into the lay-by overlooking Rock Edge and surveyed the scene. By God, what a desolate hole of a place to grow up in. No wonder teenaged Beth counted the days until she could leave. He opened his flask of coffee and poured out a steaming cup, glancing yet again at his mobile. She could have showed up, though.

If there was one person who could chip her way into this murder case, it was Beth. She'd lived here when it happened. She was related to the victim, to his mother, his aunts…Hmm, like heck she had a twenty-four bug! They'd be having words when she got back to work and no mistake.

A soughing wind buffeted his car. He grimaced - should've brought wellies and an anorak. Now he'd get soaked to the bone. He took another sip of coffee, letting it fizz round his veins, heat up his muscles ready for the day ahead.

Directly opposite the lay-by, stood the pit head - an eerie black scarecrow floating in the fog. He pictured Beth's mother - standing out here at dawn in all weathers, waiting for the bus to take her to a cleaning job in town. Howling winds, sideways sleet, rolling mists…Beth and little Alice must have been able to see her from their bedroom window.

The upper floors of the three terraces, which huddled together like whispering schoolgirls, were just about visible - a wisp of smoke curling into the dawning sky from the nearest chimney. Old Violet presumably. Beth's grandma. No fuss. And no report of her son, Adam, missing…why?

***

Beth woke up with a thump of panic - 8 a.m. -

grabbed her phone and grimaced. Three messages all from Phil, her boss. Regretting now that she'd sent him a text in the early hours - the ones she'd spent pacing up and down the living room wrapped in a blanket - saying she had a virus. A stomach bug. A cold. How lame a lie it seemed now - in the piercing light of day. The headache had been real enough though - headache from insomnia, hand-wringing worry, bad dreams - and for that she'd taken a near lethal concoction of tablets, only to fall fast asleep for three whole hours and then wake with another, bigger headache. Great. So now what?

    She threw back the covers and sat on the edge of the bed. *Think.* Well, now at least it was a given fact - this murder *did* have something to do with her. Her subconscious had been trying to tell her and she hadn't listened. So what did her subconscious know that her conscious mind didn't? Was it so awful she'd blocked it out completely? Could it be...oh surely not....Heat rose in her face. *Had she committed the murder herself? Was she a murderer?* Did Phil think that? He could do - quite reasonably.

    Beth closed her eyes and concentrated solely on breathing - *in and out, in and out* - until she had control again. Phil wouldn't believe her excuse of being sick either. And now he knew she was actually related to the victim, had lived next door at the time of his disappearance, and only yesterday sworn on her life he was still alive....Well it didn't look good, did it? So that was something else to worry about. Her job, her flat, everything she had carefully built to protect herself from ever having to go back home. And there was no safety net. She was on her own.

Stepping into the shower, she tried to massage away the heaviness thudding in her head. How long before she'd be brought into the interview room for questioning? Grilled until she tore out her own hair? Yet no matter how hard she tried to remember something - anything - there was nothing in her memory bank, not a flicker of recollection to help herself...As far as she knew Adam really did run a landscape gardening business in Leeds. Grandma Violet talked about him when she rang home, said he came to visit regularly and had recently been trying to persuade her into a nursing home.

She'd had no interest in Adam - never had since she left and particularly since Mum died. It was history. A world long ago left behind. He a relative she simply never saw. It happened. She worked with people who didn't see their own parents so to not see an uncle...and they'd never been close...

Ringing Violet now and then, though - well she was her grandma and that was different. The last call had been just a few weeks ago: *Was she okay? Yes, Adam took care of everything. She still missed 'our' Margaret. Nell and Hurry were fit and well in Scarborough, just the same, thank you*...That sort of thing...humdrum...reality...fiction. What?

The headache thumped on, shrouding her thought processes. She tipped back her head to rinse away the foam, totally unprepared for the sudden, blinding flash of clarity... Adam! There he was as plain as day - a teenager - blinking at her from behind his NHS spectacles. Winter. The Cure was playing on the record player in his room. She sitting on the window sill looking out at the pit wheel, he working at his desk. He'd turned to look at her when she'd mentioned Alice. How, she'd been wondering, could Nell be so horrid to her own daughter? Alice, who was round at their house again because Nell had locked her out in the yard.

"How can Nell abandon her like that?" she said.

"Well it's not like she..." And then he stopped himself.

"What?"

"Nothing." He shrugged, but not before she'd seen a dark cloud skitter back behind his hugely magnified eyes.

The image vanished as quickly as it had appeared.

Beth screwed up her eyes trying in vain to recall it. *It's not like she...*what? What? Oh it was so infuriating - a tantalising porthole to the past now firmly shut again. Why hadn't she tackled him about it? But of course her thoughts had been lost to Richie, hadn't they?...'*It's Friday I'm in love...*'

At least one more fact was now clear: Adam had known about something. He'd known something she hadn't, and she should have had it out of him but didn't.

Beth stepped out of the shower and grabbed a towel. She had to get to the bottom of this before Phil did. Because she herself was implicated. Yesterday she hadn't been. Yesterday it was just another case involving someone else. Today was a whole new world, and Phil was as sharp as they came. No doubt he'd get D.C. Marie Bell on the case instead of her now. Oh there'd be nothing worse than that hard as nuts little piece going through all her personal affairs. Smirking. Because little Marie with her gym-honed body and neat blonde bob - smirked!

Quickly she rubbed at her hair and dashed into the bedroom, snatching at underwear, tights and trousers. *Hurry, hurry, hurry…* The truth. Information was all. She had to get to where Adam lived: May's Landscape Gardening Business in Leeds - she sent cards there every Christmas for goodness sake.

A quick glance at her watch - about now Phil would be knocking on Violet's door for information - and then her own - there wasn't much time.

***

The trek across to the pit head had been further and taken longer than he'd thought, ruining his leather shoes - sucking footprints into the peat; damp air coating his thin jacket; sweat clammy now against his hot skin. Back in town there were daffodils quivering along the roadsides, people had their car windows down, radios playing. Like Beth always said - it really was a different world out here.

All those years he'd spent working with her

- hours staking out warehouses sipping coffee, discussing cases over a pint in the White Horse - times when working together had crossed the line into ...*What could be...What might be...*Beth's emerald eyes flashing warning lights when they'd strayed onto his turbulent divorce or her latest relationship, their gazes flicking away rapidly. Subjects changed.

Yet now here he was, standing on her grandmas's porch, aware of the nets twitching upstairs - the whistling winds through the mine shafts just as she'd described them, the cloying dampness, the desolation - now he was under her skin. He knew her, and yet there was a secret locked in here. A bad one wrapped up very tightly. So tightly she probably didn't even know it herself.

The chimney smoke meant there must be warmth inside. Phil rubbed his hands together and stamped his feet, wishing he hadn't left his car at the end of the lane. Then rapped on Violet's glass panelled front door.

It opened a couple of inches.

Phil looked down at a small, walnut-faced woman fighting with multi-coloured plastic ribbons that blew around her face. She was wearing a flowery apron and stout walking boots. "Oh aye?" she said suspiciously.

He showed his I.D. card. "D.I. Blackmore. May I come in?"

She stood aside. "'appen you're going to any road."

There wasn't much heat from the fire,

which he gravitated towards, it being the sort of fire that burned the person in front of it while blowing soot across the room and failing to warm the icy corners. Phil stood with his back to it, hoping it would take the chill off.

It was doubtful Violet's living arrangements had changed since she first moved in: a small table covered in a waxed cloth was pushed against the far wall, on top of it the remains of a meagre breakfast. He chanced it, "Any tea in that pot?"

The old lady muttered to herself as she fetched an extra cup, pouring him as strong a brew as he'd ever seen - steaming hot, tar black with full cream milk. "That do you?"

Thanking her, Phil gulped as it burned its way down his oesophagus, and then took a deep breath. There would be no easy way of saying this. "I'm here about your son, Mrs May."

Violet started dusting the room. "Wants me to go into a nursing home. Says I can't cope now I'm t' only one up here. Used to 'ave my daughters next door, and my grandchildren. Mind you - 'ad 'usband once, and all."

"Adam, Mrs May. We need to talk about Adam."

"They all left you know? Nell and Harry, then Beth and Alice, and then Margaret. Worked herself to death, my Margaret. Lost her 'usband down t' mine same as me but so young 'e were…too young. She never 'ad a proper life. And with Nell's girl to look after too. Nell were a wrong-un in them days. Just upped and left, she did. Told us it were a breakdown." She raised her eyes to the heavens. "Breakdown."

"You say Adam wants you to go into a nursing home, Mrs May? So you've seen him recently then?"

Violet narrowed her eyes. "I shan't be telling you owt, Mister."

"About what?"

"Owt."

"Do you know where Adam is?"

"Why? What's 'e done?"

"Mrs May - I take it you believe Adam is still alive?"

Violet stared at him. "Well of course 'e is. 'Ee's coming today to take me to another ruddy nursing home. Show me round - no commitment 'e says. If I don't like it I don't have to go and all that codswallop. 'e wants to sell t' terrace. I own all three you see - well my 'usband did, and now it's me. God knows who'd want to live up 'ere though? I *'ave* to mind…"

"Why? Why do you *have* to?"

There was a long pause before she answered. "Now look what's 'appened - you've gone and made me tell you summat."

Phil put down his cup on the mantelpiece. "Your granddaughter, Beth - we work together. You ever see Beth?"

Again she eyed him. "Left when she were sixteen and never came back. Saw her at Margaret's funeral that's all. She does phone though - aye, she does phone."

"And Adam?"

"Like I said - he visits regular. He'll be 'ere soon."

"Mind if I wait? Only I'd really like to meet him."

Violet started dusting again. "I'll tell 'im you were 'ere -will that do?"

"Why does this son of yours want you to go into a nursing home, Violet? May I call you Violet? Only it seems to me this is your home and you're coping pretty well, and if you're happy…"

She shrugged. "He's taken me out every day to see this one and that…some of 'em are miles away. I've kept saying I don't want to go anywhere. I just want a bit of company."

So she didn't know about the discovery of a body in the mine, then? She would have, if she'd been at home. And no one, it seemed, had told her. Did her son know? Whoever he was? Apparently not. Well, she was an old lady and he'd have to handle this very carefully.

"What are your son's plans for the terraces, Violet?"

"Razing 'em to t'ground Mister. Says no one should be living up 'ere. Wouldn't rent the others even when I begged him after Margaret died. I just wanted company and it's not like I can leave. I can never leave, you see …" She indicated the top of the pit wheel, just visible from her living room. "My husband's grave, Officer."

※ ※ ※

8.50 a.m.

Beth ignored the phone flashing Phil's name on its tiny screen. He would have been to Rock Edge by now. Spoken to her grandma. This could not be happening - had she herself killed Adam? What about that day she was convinced a ghost was chasing her in the snowstorm? The day Nell and Harry left and Alice moved in with them - Alice eating toast by the fire when she burst in with her cheeks rosy red, lungs on fire? Had she just pushed Adam down the mine shaft on her way home from school? Or seen someone else do it? Had there been another person up there? Behind the lurching yeti coming towards her?

One of her family must know something that might help her - Gran insisting Adam was alive and yet they now knew he most definitely wasn't. What was going on there? Why was she hiding vital information? It was imperative she have the chance to speak to Violet as soon as possible, before she found herself alone and defenceless in that interview room.

Stuck in traffic at this time in the morning, it was oh so tempting to stick on the blue light and charge through it. Phil was at least an hour and a half's drive away. *Keep calm. Keep calm....But even so...Come on...come on...* Eventually the lights flicked to green and she sped off down the back streets of Leeds. Knew her way thanks to her job over the years. Until finally she reached the suburbs and the address she'd always sent her Christmas cards to: May's Landscape Gardening Business should be here.

She swung the car into the cul-de-sac and

scanned the area. The no-through-road was a horse-shoe of residential bungalows with neat lawns. With the No. 7 for the Garden Centre, the only thing she could do was knock on the door. A solid ginger cat sat on the window sill looking out at her unblinkingly. She walked round the back. No one home.

As she walked back around to the front, a neighbour drew up in a white hatchback, staring at her. "Can I help you?"

"I'm looking for Adam May. Or May's Garden Business?"

The man shook his head. "Never 'eard of 'im, luv. Sorry. No - sure it's No. 7 you want?"

She nodded.

"No, it's a Mrs Parsons what lives, luv. On her own now, poor soul. We do what we can for her like…"

Beth sighed in despair. How easily people gave away information.

Back in the warmth of her car, she checked and re-checked the postcode and the map. There was no other part of the city with this road name. Yet this was where she'd sent her cards for years now. Should she stake it out? Give it some time and see who turned up? Although if the bloke next door said it was a Mrs Parsons then she could be wasting her time with that. Seemed poor Mrs Parsons got Christmas cards every year from a stranger called Beth!

But why would Violet lie to her? Did Violet know Adam had been murdered? Or was she being duped too? Because Violet couldn't drive and would never turn up to check. Did poor old Mrs Parsons get annual cards from, 'Your loving mother' too?

Her mobile shrilled, making her heart jump. She picked it up to see a text message from Phil: 'On my way to Adam's address in Leeds. How are you feeling? Meet me there? Or shall I pick you up?'

Okay, think rationally. What about Uncle Harry and Auntie Nell? *Think hard.* They'd left little Alice banging on the window that day of the white-out. The very same day she'd run home and found Alice eating toast by the fire when she got home. Was there a connection? If Nell and Harry had left an hour earlier as her mother, Margaret said, and then they were out of the picture. Already gone when she arrived home from school. Which left herself as the only suspect. Again.

But Nell and Harry might know something. Anything that would help her case. It was crucial she build up a picture of that day. Because it *was* that day when something happened. The only day on which anything happened at all. Had she seen Adam *after* that day in fact? Gone back to school? Or onto college? She started up the engine. First establish the facts. So - Scarborough it was then.

By the time she arrived there was a fresh wind blowing off the North Sea and the Scarborough crowds had already deserted the promenade. It took a while to find Nell's address, but she finally located the terraced house, very similar to the one at Rock Edge - albeit with a view of the sea instead of the moors.

It wasn't an easy prospect - visiting Auntie Nell. She'd always had a temper and even now the sound of Nell's voice through the walls - chastising, snapping, shouting and threatening, still chimed in her ears. Alice was always wailing in those days - her cheeks permanently tracked with tears, her huge green eyes brimming with misery. Harry? A great lumbering bloke she barely knew. With a funny leg and a built-up shoe he dragged along like a ball and chain.

Beth parked on the street outside the house just as the day was darkening. Oblongs of buttery light spread out onto the narrow street lined with cars. Curtains swished shut. Cats meowed to be let in. For a while she sat and stared at the house containing her long lost aunt and uncle. Mum had kept in touch with Nell, but in all other ways the claustrophobic contact of the past had been eradicated.

No. 11 was where Nell lived as far as she knew. But would the same thing happen as before? No knowledge of her existence by the neighbours?

As she hesitated, another message beeped onto her mobile phone. Phil. 'Beth. U have to come back 2 the station. Now. Address U gave 4 Adam does not exist. U R off the case!"

Someone at No. 11 drew the downstairs curtains. An older lady with a tight, white perm. Something in Beth's heart leapt as she walked up to the door. Here she would find answers.

With one knock the door flew open. Sharp blackbird eyes looked back at her. "Now then. Beth. I wondered when you'd show up," said

Auntie Nell.

***

Part 3

Phil called D.C. Bell into his office. He didn't look up from the computer screen. "Marie - I want you to find D.C. Beth Porter. Phone her every five minutes. Track her down."

"May I ask what..."

He tore a sheet off his notepad. "I'm guessing this is where she'll be."

"But this is Scarborough," Marie wailed.

"And?"

She couldn't help her glance sliding to the clock on the wall. "Nothing, Sir."

"Excellent."

He called after her as she turned to leave, "Oh and Marie? Arrest her if necessary - obstructing a murder investigation. Just get her back here as soon as possible."

The moment she shut the door he pushed the computer away and rested his head in his hands. This had to be one of the most bizarre twenty-four hours he'd ever experienced. Beth...of all people! She hadn't murdered her uncle - he was as sure of that now as he could be. She was as clueless as he was, and probably frightened half to death thinking she'd done it.

He'd waited with Violet for hours for this so-called son of hers to turn up, but in the end she'd become as agitated as he had, so he'd decided to leave his card and ask her to call him when he showed his face. Was she calling his bluff - hoping the duplicate son would spot the police car and drive away?

During the time he'd spent waiting, listening to the sharp winds rattling the windows and the fire spit, he'd come to a decision about Violet. He'd told her a body had been found in the mine and they needed to question everyone in the area. That Violet was deceiving everyone and possibly even herself meant the news it was Adam would have to be broken to her gently in case of some kind of breakdown, although where she thought the real Adam was, had to be anyone's guess. And who on earth was this man posing as her son? This son who was so keen to raze the place to the ground.

Frustrated with the old lady's stalling tactics yet reluctant to confront without officer support, he wandered out to the car deep in thought, when a sudden glint of metal caught his eye. Some way off - parked in a gateway - lurked a silver estate. The driver must have seen him at the same time, because the car suddenly u-turned and vanished quicker than Phil could fumble for his keys. Darn it. Idiot! He'd missed the plates and lost the driver in a heartbeat.

After that it had been one futile chase after another. First to Beth's. He'd fully expected her to be there - to come shiftily to the door pretending to be sniffing miserably. But her car had gone and the flat was dark. In a squeal of tyres, he headed to the next address on his list - the one Beth had provided for Adam yesterday. No one there either. Just a bewildered old lady by the name of Mrs Parsons, who had always wondered why she'd received Christmas cards from a woman called Beth.

"What about a mother?" Phil persisted. "Did you get cards from a lady calling herself Violet, or Mum?"

Mrs Parsons had shaken her head. "No. Just this Beth. It's all very odd but there's no forwarding address so I just put it up with the others, you know...she's sort of an old friend now, luv."

So Beth had been duped about Adam for thirty years. By her own grandma and her own mother? Violet must be truly frightened of this man proclaiming to be her son -so frightened she'd lied to everyone in her family.

And now Beth was out there on her own, close to finding out the family's deadly secret. What might this person do to protect themselves? Had Violet phoned her daughter, Nell, to warn her, because they all knew Beth was a police officer. A brilliant one too - the best detective he'd worked with in a very long time. She had what the others didn't - that spark of intuition, that unnervingly accurate hunch she wasn't afraid to act on.

And yet she'd missed her own family tragedy - the one right under her nose - and that could prove to be her undoing. What was clear however, was this - there were only two more players in that family, and that's probably where she'd be heading. What did her Auntie Nell and

Uncle Harry know about who was pretending to be Violet's son? Anything? Marie would hopefully be there soon and they'd find out.

Meanwhile, there was Beth's cousin, Alice. Now all grown up. He got his coat.

***

Beth ignored the repeated phone calls from Marie Bell as she drove out of Scarborough and up onto the Yorkshire moors. Stars whipped in and out of scudding clouds, and sharp gusts shook the car as it surged through the blackness. She wasn't going to start explaining things to Marie Bell of all people, especially not now when her grandma was in danger. The whole thing had sky-rocketed out of control. Call it sixth sense but she had to get to Rock Edge as fast as she could before something terrible happened.

Nell had told her precisely nothing. Eyeing her coldly from her perch on the sofa: all chintz and porcelain in a chilly front room. Like Beth, she'd left the place behind her and had no inclination to go back, she'd said. No fond memories. A demanding backward child, a mother who took her husband's wages and a drudge of a life taking in washing. When Harry had been made redundant that was the last straw - Margaret had offered to take Alice and so they'd fled while they had the chance of a new life. Surely Beth must be able to identify with that?

Beth nodded. "But I don't understand why Alice remembers things differently to you. She says you and Uncle Harry were arguing and left her banging on the window."

"Alice was a spectacularly brainless five year old."

"Nell, there's no easy way to say this - there's been a body found down the pit and the police are treating it as murder."

Nell stared. No emotion in those black eyes. Not a flicker. "And what's that to do with me? Is that why you're here? As a copper?"

Beth shook her head again. "The body's been there for thirty years. We all lived there back then and we're all being questioned. They're saying it's Adam. Violet's Adam."

"That's ridiculous."

"So you believed he was alive all this time too?"

"Of course. Lives in Leeds, doesn't he?"

Auntie Nell had listened to all Beth had to say about forensic evidence, and the fact there was no one called Adam May living at his address. Then finally she stood up. "Well, it's as much a puzzle to us as it is to you. I'll ring Mum and find out what she's been told. I'm sorry we can't be of any more help. I'll make you a cup of tea before you go."

Us…We…

While Nell was making the tea, the phone had rung in the hall, and Beth strained to hear as Nell hurried back into the kitchen, hissing furiously at whoever it was.

"Is everything okay?" she asked when her aunt returned.

Nell waved the call away as unimportant.

"Just a friend."

A moment passed. The clock ticking on the mantelpiece.

"Well, it's been a long time," said Beth, taking a grateful sip. "How is Uncle Harry? Is he around?"

"No, he's out."

"Working or…?"

"Just out," said Nell.

It was only as she'd headed out of town that the click-click-click of a new thought process had begun. Violet was duping them all into believing someone was her son when she knew he wasn't. Couldn't be. Either that or she had been frightened into duping everyone. Why? And Nell's story didn't tally with Alice's or her own mother's when she was alive. Harry was not at home. Nell and Harry did know something more, she was sure of it. And then there was that phone call - who was it with?

Harry was not at home…
Violet was alone…
Beth put her foot down.

***

Phil picked up the message from Marie on his way back from Alice's. Alice and her husband had been most helpful. There was no reason to disbelieve her account of what had happened the day she was abandoned by her parents. An event which had traumatised her for years and several times resulted in her being hospitalised. Had Beth known all this? He'd asked Alice.

Alice had shaken her head. "She'd been coming to see me the day before yesterday - she comes once a month - and I had so much to tell her. I've been having this new therapy and started to remember what I heard them say through the walls that day. I wanted to tell her but I expect it can wait."

Phil shook his head. God, the irony of it. So much Beth didn't know about her own family, and as the pieces began to slot in place, so he was closing in on the murder. Beth. Where the heck was she?

Sighing, he tapped into the latest message from Marie. Oh great! She'd missed Beth by about an hour according to Nell, who had refused to open the door. And Marie was now going home.

Going home! For God's sake they were closing in on a murderer!

He started up the engine. Educated guess: Beth would be going to her grandma's. Of course. There was no place left for her to go.

***

Beth arrived at Rock Edge as night settled in a dense, black blanket. No street lights. No stars. You couldn't see the hand in front of you.

She parked at the end of the lane and locked the car. If her intuition was right then the person who was persecuting her grandma would be with her now - having been told that Adam's body had been found. This charade had been going on for years. Whoever it was, possibly Harry, now had his back against the wall. Ideally she should have back-up. Should have told Phil she was here. Still - too late now.

Head down, she picked her way carefully along the muddy, pot-holed lane, pushing her hair out of her eyes, stumbling and cursing. However had she done this as a teenager in high heels? Drainpipe to bus stop in twenty minutes!

Suddenly Violet's end terrace was in view - the thick, stone wall staunch against the wind and spattering rain. She scanned the area. Something else - the shadow of a car - a silver estate she didn't recognise. Beth bobbed down and held her breath. He was here then. Inside.

She memorised the plate and then snuck around the back, working on instinct and hoping the windows hadn't been changed since she used to shin down the drainpipes as a teenager. What she used to do back then was wrench open the sash in the bathroom when she returned in the early hours. It was easy and all three were identical.

It worked. Dripping wet, limbs trembling, Beth broke into the bathroom and thudded onto the cold linoleum floor. Voices downstairs.

Tip-toeing along the landing she poised at the top of the stairs to listen. One man. And the unmistakeable voice of her grandma. Got to give it to her - she seemed to be holding her own in one heck of a row.

No, Gran don't goad him...

"You're telling me this now?" said the male voice. "That Adam weren't yours? I've been like a son to you because of all this. Because of what she made me do. It were bad enough to find out about Beth but…"

"I told you she were a bad 'un right from the start. If 'er own mother told you that then you'd 'ave to be I don't know what to carry it on."

"So what happened with Adam then? Who…?"

"Who were t' father? I don't know, Lad. I said I'd take him because she were just a teenager and she hated all t' gossip. And then Margaret took Beth, of course."

Beth, listening upstairs, gasped and clamped her hand over her mouth.

"Did you 'ear owt just then?" said Violet.

"No. Look, I only found out about Beth being mine that day we left. We were rowing about Alice and what a miserable life Nell was having to endure because of being married to me, and then suddenly she told me *that* - taunted me that I'd been living next door to my own child and never known. She didn't want any of 'em. I told her she could go but no way was I leaving my two girls. We had this massive fight."

"And then what really 'appened? Come on - tell me the truth. I think I deserve it, don't you?"

Suddenly they stopped talking. Turned.

Beth walked down the stairs and looked from one to the other.

Violet slumped into a chair.

Harry blanched.

"Come on then, Harry. Tell us - how exactly did you murder my brother?"

He seemed to sink. Crumple as a man.

"I had to see you."

"So what happened to Adam?"

Suddenly there was a loud bang on the front door and it crashed in off its hinges. Phil stood there, panting as if he'd run a marathon. "Yes Harry, I'd like to know too. How exactly did you kill Beth's brother, Adam?"

Harry shook his head. "I didn't," he said. "It was Nell. I'm sorry Violet - she made me take the blame, said no one would believe it could be her with her being so small and me a big lumbering bloke. I spent half my life trying to make it up to you. Couldn't tell you. I'm so sorry."

***

Hours later, Phil and Beth sat in his car eating burgers as the sun came up.

"How did you know I was there?" she asked.

"I went to see Alice."

Beth nearly choked on her burger. "You did what? She's not well, Phil. You can't - it's all delicate therapy - one minute she's not herself and the next she seems fine. You can't…"

"Well I did. Her husband was there and she was fine about it. She'd been waiting to see you the other day when you didn't turn up, to tell you about her new diagnosis and the treatment she'd been having. She remembers more than she'd told you before. Recalls hearing her parents rowing - her mother yelling that Beth was his daughter and he was going to lose them both - it was either her or you two because she didn't want either of you, she wanted out for good."

"So my mum wasn't my mum."

He reached across to take her hand. "Oh I think she was - in every way that mattered. Just as she was to your sister, Alice."

"My sister…"

"And Violet was to your brother, Adam."

A tear dripped down Beth's cheek. "I have to sort out a decent funeral for him, you know? I think Violet would want that too."

"Take all the time you need. The three of you have a lot of grieving and catching up to do."

"I still don't get how it happened. Why Adam was up there."

"Maybe Nell will tell us in court."

A picture of Nell's darting blackbird eyes popped into Beth's mind. "Maybe it really was an accident. I mean - there was no reason for Nell to hate Adam, was there?"

"Hmm…Alice said something about her mother saying 'he' over and over again. 'He' was old enough to go to the pub and spread rumours."

"Was she really so afraid of local gossip?"

"Seem she hated it. But there was still no reason for her to hate her own son. No, it must have been an accident like Harry said - she can't be that evil. Although I still think she'll blame the lot on Harry."

"My dad." Beth frowned. "I don't think I can call him that."

"He came for you, though. He wasn't going to leave Alice and he wasn't going to leave you.

Or even Violet - he was going to take care of all of you. Nell trapped him."

"Do you believe that?"

"I think he was telling the truth, yes. It ties in with what Alice said too. Harry said she could clear off but he was staying and taking care of his children. Nell drove off and Harry went up to meet you - to tell you what had happened and explain that Alice and you were going to be taken care of. He planned to take care of Margaret too - knowing how hard her life was. Only Nell saw him from the road, and here's my hypothesis: her car was stuck again and she was out with the spade. In a fit of temper she walked out to remonstrate with him some more - only it seemed somehow Adam stepped into the frame and she hit him instead of Harry by mistake. Then she and Harry went back to tell Violet there'd been an accident, that Harry had accidentally hit Adam, and between the three of them they decided to keep it in the family. Harry would take care of Violet and the pretence began."

Beth nodded. "So Alice would have been taken to Mum's, and I would have arrived home to find her there. I bet Mum never knew any different and Alice's story would have made perfect sense. No wonder Nell and Harry didn't want anyone else living up there and then the terraces razed to the ground. They almost got their wish, too. A few more weeks and that place would have been deserted forever - and so would Adam."

"If it hadn't been for that bloke and his Jack Russell - yes."

Beth nodded and wiped her eyes. "I'm glad you came looking for me. You worked all night!"

Phil smiled into her eyes and this time neither of them looked away. "You'd do the same for me."

"Of course."

He reached for her hand and she smiled back at him.

"Look," said Phil. "You take all the time you need to give Adam the burial he deserves, okay? And when you're feeling up to it, well - how about that pie and a pint some time?"

"Ooh you big romantic!"

Phil laughed. "So it's a yes then?"

"It's definitely a yes," said Beth. "One thing I don't understand, though, Phil. And we must get to the bottom of it. What was Adam doing up at the pit in that weather? Why was he there?"

Phil put his arm around her, pulled her close. "I guess there are some things we'll never know. He can't tell us, can he?"

***

1983

The bus choked and stalled on the hill up to Rock Edge, eventually sliding sideways across the lane. The driver turned to look at his sole passenger. "Sorry, Kid - you'll 'ave to walk rest o' t' way."

Adam grabbed his school bag and jumped off into the swirling snowstorm. Head down against the prevailing winds, he tramped steadily towards the top of the hill. Already his specs were covered in snow and his ears screamed with freezing pain. Once at the bus stop he could see the three chimneys of home - smoke spiralling into the snowy sky - and it was then he noticed a car abandoned. That was Harry's car - a Vauxhall that had seen better days. Had it broken down again? They should have asked him - he was great with cars.

It was then he heard voices and turned in their direction. Blimey, was Nell out there? In a long coat and boots? Trying to get the attention of someone to help her with the car? He squinted into the snowstorm. And made a decision. He'd go and help her.

Tramping towards the pit head, the blizzard blew ever stronger until he couldn't see anything at all, turning around and around to get his bearings. Nell in front - nearer - still holding her spade. He held out his hands. "Nell - give me the spade! I'll help you."

Obviously she hadn't heard. She was marching towards the figure in the distance. Shouting. He tried again, shouting louder this time. "It's okay - Nell - It's Adam. Give me the..."

Suddenly she swung round. A pause while her dark eyes pierced into his own. Her voice was shrill and he struggled to catch the gist, "It's all your fault this - folk all know and I 'ave to leave... losing my 'usband - All t' gossip.... out now ....and he's telling 'er!"

She lifted the spade high into the air.

Blackness. Falling. The faraway sound of a man's voice, Harry…. ?

"God, Nell - what have you done?"

The shrieking sound of a woman, fainter now, "What do you mean, what have *I* done?" Laughing… "What have *you* done, Harry? What have *you* done?"

And then there was nothing.

Nothing for thirty years - except the haunting cries of long-buried miners sighing through the tunnels. And catching in the wind.

THE END

1. Published by Woman's Weekly 2013

3. Rough Love

The front door slams. He leaves me crumpled on the stairs, staring bleak-eyed at the empty space he filled moments before: pointing, accusing, his beautiful mouth carved into a line of ugly contempt. But still there, imprinted on my world. And now he's gone.

Jay. A man impossible to second guess - from thunderous expression to disarming smile, soft caresses to an iron grip. His hungry stare lingers, haunting me, his steel embrace and panting breath hot on my neck...... Hot tears roll towards my ears, stinging, melting into my hair. So that's it. Over with one last slam. A slam so violent it makes the thin house tremble, a little more damp wallpaper slide down the walls and the bare light bulbs sway and flicker. How long I sit there I don't know. Cars whoosh past, spraying the pavements with diesel painted puddles, shadows play on the walls with the streetlights, and a long, long time later - the air around me darkens and chills.

The sheets are cold when I crawl in. They smell musty and faintly, ever so faintly, of Jay. Lying still and numb I stare with wide, sore eyes at the changing shapes on the ceiling - at blues and blacks and greys. A car door bangs, there's shouting in the street, a dustbin lid crashes. Sometime around dawn, as ethereal fingers begin to poke through the slats of heavy cloud, a catfight pierces the silent gloom. Later, there are footsteps and a remote clicks open a car door. Gear changes fade into the distance. Perhaps I drift off - bizarre dreams tainted with an emotion I don't remember but which leaves me disturbed - but now there is more light. Doors open and close nearby. Newspapers snap through letterboxes. Another day. A day without him. Then another and another. The nights will be the worst.

"You need to see a doctor, Danielle," says my mother.

She's standing next to my bed with a cigarette hanging from her lower lip, arms folded. So she's back then from wherever she's been this time. She's got Kieren and Liam with her, I can hear them running rampage downstairs and tinkling animation coming from the TV. She reeks of nicotine and crisps and cheap perfume. "It's no good turning away from me. Look at the state of you. You need help. It's not right, this isn't. Anyway, I've brought us some chips if you want some."

"I don't need a doctor." It's strange to speak, tongue and lips tripping over the words. "I just need time."

She turns to stare out of the window and takes a deep drag of her cigarette. The light is harsh, highlighting the crevices on either side of her mouth and around her eyes, her complexion sallow and lifeless. Her body is thin and rangy like mine, only kind of used-up looking and too stringy for the tight jeans and skimpy top she's wearing. The hair is yellow with black roots, like partially burnt corn, the heels of her cowboy boots worn down, nails bitten and hands as gnarled as ancient tree roots. "Time," she says, as if seriously contemplating what I just said. She turns round. "I'm going down for my chips. They'll be on the table in two minutes if you want some. Either that or starve. It's up to you, Danielle."

***

A long time after winter drags itself into the early days of spring, and bare branches forked against grey transform into shivering green arms, I open my bedroom window and lean out, breathing in the new air - earthy and slightly sweet mingled with petrol. I've spent my days and weeks spilling out of bed onto the sofa downstairs, trawling through shopping channels on the TV with glassy eyes, swilling bottled drinks then dragging myself back upstairs again. Music thumps through the walls and the boys fight like tigers. My mum's got a new boyfriend, Keith. I can hear the bed creaking again at night, muffled giggles and his mobile going off with its stupid frog tune. Always here with his big feet on the table, his bald pate shining in the light from the TV and his hairy hands on the remote. Outside, kids hang around in the street, cars rev, and life plays out around me, as if the shape that is me wouldn't matter if it was coloured-in or not.

This morning, though, there's something different. Maybe it's the green shoots sprouting through the scruffy bit of lawn outside my window, the distant shouts from the schoolyard, or perhaps it's just time - the time I needed - but I want to go out. And now I've decided, I have to go. As I leave I catch sight of myself in the hall mirror - thin and ashen-faced, with a cheap pink anorak pulled over tracksuit bottoms and my hair scraped back in a ponytail. A walking stereotype.

The park is almost deserted. Litter flutters in tiny piles, flirting around bins loaded with cans and bags full of 'doggy-do' as little Liam calls them. Pit bulls mostly, round here. At this time of day the hooded teens are fast asleep and the only visitors are single mothers pushing buggies, their eyes hollow with exhaustion and hopelessness. I find a bench near the pond and sit down, ignoring the icy chill on my back, lifting my face to the weak rays of sunshine. If only Jude was here, my so called best friend who called round just once, said I was a 'Saddo' who needed to 'get a life.' It's like she's deleted me and there's nothing I can do about it.

A shout snaps me back and instantly I'm on alert. But it's only a woman chasing an errant puppy. The puppy is a chubby black and white spaniel with his tail held importantly high, eyes bright. He's chasing a leaf as it first rustles along the path hen lifts into the air, twizzling round and round, dancing in the sunshine just out of his reach. The puppy pounces, misses, leaps and misses again. He spins around as finally the leaf floats away on a breeze, watching mesmerised and bemused, lost in his sweet and simple world. He had it and now he doesn't. Our eyes lock - his wide and brown and full of warmth and spirit - and something connects.   Then the woman reaches him, clips on a lead and the moment is gone. A moment that shifts the axis of my world so completely it is as if a switch has been flicked. "Come on Harry, you naughty boy. I don't know. I let you off the lead for just one minute and….."

He glances back at me and I smile. Smile. For the first time in God knows how long. Because now I can see, really see. No one, I'm thinking, no one has the right to take purity and innocence, and turn it into despair.

***

The rage when it erupts is savage and vicious. "How dare you?" I shout, banging doors and pounding up the stairs.

She comes after me. "I'm in trouble because of you, Danielle. You're a bloody monster. I'm in court because of you."

She flicks ash on my bed and I swipe it off. I bare my teeth and spew my venom while she tries to slap me, over and over. Like she slapped me when I told her about Jay, when she didn't believe me, when she said I was a liar and a tart and a home-wrecker.

"Haven't you got to pick up Liam from nursery?"

She glares at me, forced to look at her watch. "I'll get Kerry to go from next door. You….." She points at me. "You need sorting."

It is two days later when I find out what this means. She's waiting for me when I get home from wandering round the park. We've had hail and sleet, my hands are mottled with purple and my lips are frozen. She is standing with her hands on her hips in the hallway, eyes narrowed to slits.

"Now you're fourteen, Danielle, it's been decided. You're going to your nan's to live."

I stare back at this woman who is my mother. Into the face that is sculpted, partly by character but mostly by experience, into aggression and defiance. She lifts her cigarette to her lips and inhales deeply, blowing a plume of smoke at the yellowing ceiling.

"You can get the bus this afternoon. I've packed your stuff. Maybe she can get you to go to school because I can't do a bloody thing with you and I'm in enough trouble as it is. I've given up, washed my hands of you, Danielle. I've got Kieran and Liam to think of now."

Not to mention Keith, I think, who's parked himself on our sofa to watch the racing while Liam sits eating a greasy packet of crisps for his lunch.   My Nan has a one-bedroom maisonette with cardboard thin walls and the windows boarded up at the back because of repeated break-ins. A gang of yobs hang around outside on the triangle of mud that passes for a Green, burning tyres and swilling cider, threatening, jeering and intimidating those who fear them. Nan has a panic alarm and rarely leaves her home.

I stare into my mother's eyes and realise she doesn't give a damn. But it doesn't matter anymore: it's not her fault, not mine, not anyone's, just how it is. Wordlessly I shrug and clomp upstairs for the last time, pick up my holdall containing the few possessions I have and let myself out.

Needles of sleety rain sting my cheeks as I wait for the bus. I stamp my feet and I'm thinking - my life can go one of several ways now. I can get this bus or cross the road and get another. It rounds the corner, trundling towards me. Decision time. Seconds to go. Shall I get on it or not?
Nan will be waiting for me. Twitching the nets every few minutes. Probably she's made a cake and cooked a meal. My makeshift bed will be made up with clean sheets. And she doesn't' bring home tattooed men who swig from cans all day and creep into my bedroom at night. Telling me they love me. Messing with my head. The bus screeches to a halt, the doors hiss open, and I get on it.

THE END

Rough Love was first published by:
1. Debut, Park Publications, UK. Summer 2009
2. Ether books.com 2011

4. Cold Melon Tart

When I first saw Leo I did what everyone does - I flinched. It was like catching sight of someone reflected in the hall of mirrors. Poor guy, but then he must have become used to it over the years. All those double takes, frank stares and nudged ribs. *Look at him. Oh my God. Have you seen that*?

"Two espressos and a piece of your delicious melon tart, please," he said. Then, squinting at my name badge. "Thank you, Lucy."

"That's okay. Hot or cold?"

"Oh, cold."

I recovered myself quite well, I thought. Possibly because of the near murderous glare of the woman he was with. While he paid, he told her to find a table, that he'd bring everything over. "Are you sure you don't want anything to eat?" he asked.

She pressed her lips together and gave a firm, little shake of her head before clattering off to a table in the far corner on ridiculous high heels. Ridiculous because her companion was so very short. Said a lot about her, those heels.

"So, you're new here?" he asked, over the hiss of the espresso machine.

I nodded, keeping the fixed grin on my face, trying not to stare. Just talk normally. "First day."

He paid and took the tray. "Don't worry, I'm sure you'll be fine. I can tell." Martha, who was busy grinding coffee beans, shouted over her shoulder in mock horror. "Of course she will. I don't take on idiots, you know."

"I'm Leo, by the way," he said. "Everyone knows me. Once seen never forgotten, isn't that right, Martha?" His laugh rang hollow, tinkling in my head like ghostly children in an empty house.

From then on I saw him regularly. The thing was, I'd never come across anyone like him before. Ever. Oh, at school there'd been this boy who had to wear a wig and all the kids used to chant 'Wiggy' at him on the walk home. And in my class at University there's this girl with MS called Clare. But Clare's pretty and clever and doted on by everyone. The boys fall over themselves to carry her things and she has a specially adapted car and gorgeous clothes.

I looked down at the cheap black skirt I'd found in the sales, wiped my hands on the hugely unflattering red, checked apron I had to wear, and figured that we all had our burdens. Mine was paying for my education, hoping no one had stolen the food I'd bought from out of the fridge when I finally got back to the dingy terrace I shared, or nicked my drying underwear off the radiators. But nothing, nothing could be worse than Leo's burden. To have to live like that…

Usually Leo came in alone, sometimes with the woman I now knew as Tina. He always paid. No cover girl herself, she didn't treat him all that nicely, and it seemed to me that he was pitifully grateful to have her around at all. And she knew it. Covertly I'd sneak a glance at them while I cleared tables. He'd be chatting and she'd be staring at some place over his shoulder, not making any attempt to even pretend she was listening. I began to wonder if she was a resentful relative until I saw him reach for her hand one day, stroking the back of it over and over as if willing her to love him. To be honest, you know what I thought? I thought - what a bitch. For sure he didn't look good but presumably she knew that when she agreed to go out with him? For goodness sake, there was a human being under there. A really, really nice one too. A gentleman. Such a change from the sullen, hyper-critical boys I knew, who talked about girls like they were items chosen from a catalogue, swigged lager and never, ever asked you a single question. Perhaps being with him made her feel better about herself, and if so then she was even more of a....You know, I could feel my pulse bouncing along my arteries.

    Maybe that's what started it. The fact that there he was, a guy not much older than me but with a warm, selfless personality despite his obvious afflictions - an innocent buffeted around by human inadequacies. Yet the barbs and taunts he must have suffered should surely have made him angry? I developed this sort of morbid fascination. Like, what *exactly* had caused his illness? And why didn't he do something about it?

    I don't remember broaching the subject outright, but one day he was there on his own pushing a piece of melon tart around on his plate when we fell into conversation. Pleasant stuff, you know - just the weather and what I was studying. I liked that about him. That he was interested in what I had to say. Then it just came out - I don't think he meant it to happen but his misery was bubbling up long before it finally spilled over. He tried to contain it but it was clear he needed a friend. "Tina's had enough." Yes. I could have told him that weeks ago.

"They all do eventually. It's the NF." He pointed to the protrusion on his forehead.

"NF?" Well, I was studying English and drama not sciences.

He smiled indulgently. "Neurofibromatosis. It's where tumours grow in the nerve tissue. There isn't a lot you can do. I've had the worst ones removed but the one on my spine and here," he indicated a large cricket ball sized lump on the back of his skull and a smaller one protruding from his right jaw. "They're too dangerous to touch."

I nodded. Okay, so now I knew what to look up on the Internet. We chatted for several minutes about how amazed he'd been when Tina, who had sold him a small studio from where he worked as an architect, had got chatting to him and let him buy her lunch one day - he still remembered it, smiling while he stirred the refill of coffee I'd just poured. It had been a warm afternoon, and the café had been beside the canal, sunshine glinting off the water. A moment of precious time, captured forever in his memory. 'Normal,' was the word he used to describe how he felt that day. '*Almost* normal.' Then he snapped back to the present. "She's just met someone new, that's all. It happens."

I patted his hand. I had so many questions to ask but somehow the words jumbled in my mouth and wouldn't line up properly.

"Sorry," he said. "I do go on."

"No, no - not at all."

The man, I realised, was watching me carefully. "I think," he said, rubbing his jaw line. "That people just change."

You know I was bursting with compassion but it was all I could do not to dissolve, to keep the pity from my eyes. If I were him I would hate that. Imagine - either revulsion or pity from everyone who laid eyes on you? But it was difficult. And even more so when, on that last time he came in with Tina, I could see that his head was down while she, not even taking off her coat or touching her coffee, sat and stared at him. It occurred to me then to wonder how it might be for them in private. Had she been mean to him? I couldn't bear it.

Frankly I was relieved when, finally, their relationship was truly over and he began to come in on his own again, even though he looked pathetically downcast. He didn't want my sympathy, just a friendly word and his coffee and melon tart. But after that, a week or so, it began to get rather tricky.

I'll try to tell it exactly as it happened, but you must understand that the blinding flash of clarity I had all but eclipsed what happened first.

Well, here goes. I was tidying up after the

lunch time rush one day, wiping down tables, clearing cups and plates, when I felt his eyes on me, following every move I made. And despite everything, the way he looked, I felt a tiny flutter of excitement. You have to realise he was an intelligent, sensitive, kind and funny man, with warm brown eyes that melted like chocolate. If it weren't for one tiny defect, a mutation of the NF1 gene, he would have been gorgeous. Well, anyway, I smiled back, one of those secretive this-is-just-between-us sort of smiles, a tacit communication that signalled complicity. And looking back there it was - that moment, that spark of pure egocentric stupidity - that one little thing we wish we hadn't done.

"Don't suppose there's any chance of a refill, is there?" he asked, indicating his empty cup.   I was due for class but I topped him up anyhow.

He smiled hopefully. "And another piece of melon tart?"

He must be feeling better, I thought, sliding the last piece onto a clean plate. That melon tart was the house speciality - short crust pastry, a custard base and dozens of honeydew melon balls crowded on top. It melted in the mouth and Leo loved it. Some people had it warmed up but it wasn't so nice that way - a bit gooey. I brought it over and we got talking, just the two of us, while Martha washed up in the back kitchen. I remember the sun streaming in through the blinds, dust mites dancing in the slanted rays, the feeling that the afternoon was running past the window, leaving me behind on the warm, plastic coated bench, dozy, hypnotised, breathing in the heady aroma of espresso and re-heated croissants.   He took a sip of coffee through the side of his distorted mouth. Turned out he'd been to see his consultant that morning.

"I've got another one coming," he explained. And for the first time I noticed a slight bulge at his left temple. "They're all growing and I've lost two more teeth on this side." Whenever he spoke the saliva flowed unchecked from the corner of his mouth causing him to dab at it constantly with a tissue. I knew by then, from researching his condition on the Internet, that things would worsen. And there was no cure.

A cold blast of air rushed across my back. Peering over my shoulder I noticed a young mother with a toddler in a pushchair. I'd turned quickly, in time to see the look of revulsion and horror that washed over her face when she caught sight of Leo.

I said, "We're shut," coldly, unpleasantly, not like me at all. Our eyes locked and I could feel protective fury rising, glaring just like Tina had at me. After she'd gone - the whole incident only lasting a couple of seconds - I swivelled back round to see Leo spooning a piece of melon tart into the side of his mouth. He struggled to keep the mixture of saliva and custard from seeping back out, and a globule of custard oozed down his chin.

"I wondered," he said, putting down his

spoon. "How you might feel about going to the theatre with me tomorrow night? I've got a spare ticket now that Tina–"Martha had switched on the extractor fan and it's loud hum filled the room. Filled my head. You see, it was by then that I knew where this was going. And I also knew, in a flash of ice-sharp clarity, sitting there in the sun-warmed booth with the clanking of crockery and the whirring fan in the background, that to my everlasting shame, I couldn't do it.

THE END

Cold Melon Tart was first published by: 1.Debut, Park Publications, 2009
2. Globalshortstories.com Online competition winner, March 2010
3. Ether books.com 2011

5. The Witching Hour

From somewhere inside the house a door slammed.

And suddenly he was wide-awake, eyes straining against a wall of blackness, heart racing. He tried to call out but no sound came from his constricted throat, and his wife slept on. Tick-tick-tick-tick…….Nothing there but the bedside clock…..and ..something else…..breathing. Not his own. Someone there. Coming closer. He tried to move but his leaden limbs were paralysed. Watching, waiting, as out of the darkness a shape formed. Climbed onto his chest. Heavy. He couldn't breathe. He was going to die and he couldn't even scream. Then came the voice, delivered mockingly, "Good morning, Jack. Wakey, wakey… It's 3am."

***

9am:

The medical receptionist looked up from her desk and gave the pretty, young drug rep a wintry smile. "Don't keep him long this morning - he's got a full clinic waiting."

Hayley Peters returned the glacial lip twitch and knocked on Dr McGowan's door. He was a nice guy, she was thinking, one of the few who offered her coffee and bothered to ask how she was keeping. Some of her other psychiatrist clients could learn a thing or two about that.

But today there was no cheery call to come on in. She knocked again. Silence. Well how odd! Cautiously Hayley pressed down the door handle and slowly nudged open the door. "Hello?"

Jack McGowan's office was a modern box piled high with books and reading material, a testament to his volume of work. He had his back to her, staring at the computer screen. A blank computer screen.

"Dr McGowan?"

Jack turned with a puzzled expression, raked his hair and rubbed his face repeatedly, then gestured to the chair opposite. "Ah, sorry Hayley - bad night." "The children?"

He looked shocking - grey pallor, red, peephole eyes - weary beyond all reason. Hayley hesitated, unsure of how to proceed. Perhaps a change of subject? "Feels like spring might be round the corner, still a bit chilly out, though," she said, reaching into her briefcase for a sales brochure.

Eventually he said, "No, It's not the kids."

"Oh? A difficult patient?"

"Sort of. Well, originally–" He tailed off, distracted, rubbing his face over and over as if deciding something. Then suddenly he poured out the story in a torrent. Something Hayley wished later, with all her heart, that he hadn't.

"It was Linda," he said. "We'll call her

Linda - just out of prison and suffering from severe depression. She'd roll up in a ball in the corner of the ward and not do a thing you asked her. Just be looking back at you wild eyed, kicking and spitting if you went near. We tried everything, Hayley. Then I had this idea - hypnosis." He paused.

Hayley waited.

"Shouldn't have."

Twenty-two year old Hayley looked around at the photos on his desk of a happy family life, of freckle-faced kids grinning at the camera, at his array of certificates on the wall, and felt an unaccountable stab of fear. This father, this doctor, this bastion of the established adult world, was broken. And about to tell her why.

***

Jack's Story:

It had been a tough decision. Linda had been in prison for many years following an armed robbery resulting in the death of a security officer. Disruptive and tormented, she had finally been sectioned, since when she had become significantly more agitated.

"I want to try hypnosis," Jack told his colleagues at the team meeting.

And soon after the first session, Linda had shown a remarkable improvement. However, less than an hour into her second session her demeanour suddenly changed. Gone the angst ridden young woman and in her place a grinning mask of pure malice. She began to speak in a deep, male voice, that called itself the Prince and began to make serious threats against Jack and his staff if they continued with this line of treatment.

To everyone's horror the Prince seemed to know every intimate detail about Jack's private life and that of his wife. Quickly realising that the demon was feeding off his energy, Jack tried to calm the situation down by meditating, and after a while the energy began to dissipate and the lights flickered. Linda became Linda again and the mask melted away. When she woke she had no recollection of what had happened and shortly afterwards, contentedly sipping tea, announced that she wanted to stop taking drugs.

But that night as Jack lay in bed turning over the day's events, the marital bed began to tremble and shake, gently at first, then quite violently. His wife remained sleeping. Jack, alarmed, switched on the lamp and immediately the bed stilled. *Bad dream*. He glanced at the clock. It was 3am.

The following morning, shortly after he arrived at work a phone call from an angry colleague was put through. "Now look here, McGowan - I'm telling you now I have no intention of carrying out this ridiculous request. Quite frankly I'm amazed you had the gall to ask."

Puzzled, Jack asked him what he was talking about - he had made no request. The other doctor insisted it had been Jack who had left the message on his personal answer phone and would not repeat it for fear of embarrassing them both further.Confused and not a little upset, Jack continued with his work before attending a lunchtime meeting. When he arrived at the meeting, however, he found his place had been cancelled earlier that morning and was refused admittance. The cancellation had been made by himself.

There were other oddities. His computer would flash up without warning, the printer would print unfathomable messages, lights dimmed and brightened and a book flew off the shelf. Then he'd picked up the phone to a caller who spoke only gibberish, except it was very clearly enunciated gibberish as if Jack should be able to understand. When he didn't the caller became extremely agitated and Jack had to put the phone down.

That night he lay awake trying to work out what was happening. Either he was losing his mind or some external force was influencing him. His wife, exhausted after her long day with the children, murmured something in her sleep and Jack sighed. He couldn't burden her with this.

Alone in the dark, his scientific mind tried to analyse the situation. But every avenue he took led him to the same conclusion: Linda's demon. He didn't want to believe it but what else could it be unless he was going insane? The demon must be inside himself instead of Linda. She was better. He, however, was being tortured.   A crash downstairs and his eyes snapped open from an exhausted sleep. The night air sat black and heavy, a suffocating blanket. Something there. Edging nearer. A weight pressing down on his chest and hot, fetid breath in his ear, its voice silky and content, "You are mine now, doctor, and just think what I can do with your patients…oh what delicious fun I'm going to have……..."

Jack tried to move his head away but found he could not. His heart was galloping, sweat pouring in rivulets down his forehead, dripping into his eyes, down his neck, soaking the pillow.

*"*We are one now, Jack. My perfect soul mate - so difficult finding the right host - evil and rotten. So important to have an….affinity…"

He wanted to scream, 'Never, never,' but no sound came. And his wife slept on. Downstairs the clock chimed. It was 3am. *The bloody witching hour again*.

***

He began to dread the nights. The big, comfy marital bed no longer the delicious sanctuary he had come to cherish.

"You look knackered," said his wife over breakfast. "We should book a holiday, Jack."

He nodded, distracted. Everything was normal. The kids were running round arguing and getting ready for school, the baby was whimpering and refusing to eat his boiled egg, the post plopped onto the mat and the radio played a familiar pop tune - '*So you had a bad day…..*'

"What about the Canary Islands?" His wife was spooning egg yolk into the mouth of their youngest child - an apple-cheeked toddler with red hair and fat fingers. "Yes, fine, book it. Oh, let me check the diary first."

"Do it today then Jack, and I'll get it sorted. Blimey, you look rough." That night he slept downstairs, afraid to drop off , but inevitably he dozed, wrapped in the duvet from the spare room while the electric fire hummed and shadows played on the walls. A loud explosion woke him. On full alert, heart thumping somewhere in his throat, the first thing he noticed was that the fire was off and the room was cold. His breath steamed on the night air. Total silence.

"Who's there?"

He wandered into the hall to find the front door wide open and a stream of freezing air rushing past him. Closed it. Locked it. Immediately the study door slammed shut. Then the kitchen door. He stood alone in the hallway, waiting. "Who's there?"

The darkness intensified. Tick-tick-tick-tick. A creaking door above him. He began to climb the stairs, overwhelmed with a feeling that something was very wrong up there. His children, his wife…

Upstairs the darkness was thicker, almost palpable. There was a light on in the bedroom. His wife reading. Unusual but maybe she couldn't sleep, that's all it was. Nothing to be worried about. He pushed open the bedroom door. But his wife was not in bed. And then he saw her. On the floor, her body cold and rigid.

After the initial shock, Jack grabbed a

blanket from the bed and covered her. Her body was set to stone and icy cold and it took every ounce of his strength to drag her to the bed and then lift and roll her back in. And another hour before he felt her muscles gradually relax. Thankfully when she woke she remembered nothing except she 'didn't feel too good.'

Things were getting worse. He had to tell someone.

***

9.30am:

Hayley listened with a mixture of disbelief and horror.

"Dr McGowan, you must get help."

Slowly he lifted his head. "Ah, Hayley, I know. I'm sorry. I shouldn't have burdened you, but–"

"It's ok, really."

He looked at her. "I couldn't tell any of my colleagues or they'd have me committed!"

Hayley smiled. How she wanted to get out of here. "Glad I came in useful - I'll expect a lot of business after this, though."

***

But all day Jack's story didn't leave her and everything went wrong. '*So you had a bad day....*'

Jack's secretary snapped at her for taking so much time. Her car wouldn't start. Her next appointment had been mysteriously cancelled and then she got a parking ticket. By the time she arrived home to find she'd lost her flat keys, she felt a cold coming on and looked forward to a bath and an early night.

She took a book to bed. The novel was a good one and, engrossed, she jumped at the sudden sound of breaking glass. Silence screamed in her ears as she strained to listen. Oh God no - someone was inside her home, footsteps clomping down the corridor. This could not be happening. She caught sight of herself in the mirror - a blonde child-faced woman reading a book beneath a pink lamp - at the expression of fear on her face. Watched in horror as an elongated shadow of a hand crept across the wall behind her. And switched off the lamp. She tried to scream but no sound came. Beside her the bedside clock glowed in the dark.

It was 3am.

THE END

The Witching Hour was first published as,'3am and Wide Awake' by Ether Books in 2011, and is the basis to the prologue of, 'Father of Lies' – an occult horror trilogy now out on Amazon in both digital and paperback formats, as well as audio.

6. Girl in the Rain

She was thumbing a lift on the A1 slip road when I first saw her: mini skirt, long, dark hair dripping down her back, tramping along in the pouring rain with a cigarette clamped between heavily ringed fingers and a rucksack on her shoulder.

Don't pick her up.

The Merc was easing into fourth and I shouldn't have stopped, but something about the kid's sopping clothes and the HGVs thundering past, showering her with muddy spray on what was a mercilessly cold, squally November night, nagged at my conscience.

"Where do you want to go?"

She shrugged, pale face bobbing through my zapped down window. "Anywhere."

She was shivering in a thin, cheap pink parka, arms hugging her chest, bare legs covered in goose pimples.

The Merc's seats were cream leather so I grabbed my Mac off the back seat and spread it for her to sit on. "I'm going as far as Darlington if that's any good to you?"

Mistake.

She nodded, stubbed out what remained of her cigarette on the wet road and slid into the warm, luxurious cocoon of my car.

"Soon have you warmed up," I said, turning up the heater as she rubbed her arms, rivulets of water running down her legs into scuffed trainers. "I'm Janine, by the way. You?"

"Leah." She smelled of chips.

"Do you like Miles Davis?"

Cool, lazy jazz snaked out of the CD player like curls of smoke, conjuring up images of the end of a party, waking bleary-eyed to find everyone else had gone and the cleaners had arrived.

Leah shrugged. "Whatever."

She'd got her texting fingers poised over the mobile she'd instantly plucked from the rucksack, leaving a trail of lip gloss, crisp packets and tissues strewn across my immaculately valeted carpet. The rain was gaining momentum, drumming methodically on the roof, wipers swatting furiously at road spray - a never-ending car wash. Leah's phone beep-beeped and she read the latest text message while dabbing at her legs with a tissue; her tiny skirt a sodden dishrag clinging to mottled thighs. "Hardly dressed for it," I said.

"Whatever."

Dan can't stand girls like her. Gum popping, cigarette sucking, monosyllabic teens who dress like hookers. The thought of him and how near I was to him - getting closer with every minute in fact - kick started my heart, taking me by surprise. People were driving too slowly. *For Christ's sake - it's only a bit of rain.*

Too close to the lorry in front, I couldn't see properly, pulled out, 70mph, up to 80, 90... I could feel Dan's rage building up already. See his face glaring out at the rain lashed night... I picked

up a hitchhiker. I'm sorry. I shouldn't have done it.
Mistake.

It had been a long day, showcasing illustrations and marketing ideas for an advertising company. My profession and I'm proud of it - gives me a sense of who I am and what I could be. But freelance. Best that way. I can only cope with one boss and that's Dan. *Never forget it. Don't ever forget.* Red taillights reflected off the road; blurred faces at windows, everyone trying to get home. Time, so little of it. Leah stopped texting and looked across at me, at my face screwed up in concentration, at my hands, claw like, on the steering wheel. "In a hurry?"

"I just have to get home, that's all."

"Husband?"

I chose to ignore her. Why should I tell her anything? None of her business. Besides, I don't talk about Dan.

"You?" I nodded towards the mobile phone she appeared to be welded to. "Boyfriend trouble?"

"Yeah, right."

"Ex-boyfriend then?"

Mistake number two. Don't get her talking.

"Shagged some stupid tart, didn't he? I mean, ohmyGod, what a total slapper!"

The rain was really coming down hard by then, pounding the car, and the last place I wanted to be in weather like that was stuck in a metal box. Locked in. Because the memories start creeping back - just me and the rain hammering on a corrugated iron roof: all night in the pitch black with spiders and webs catching at my hair, damp seeping into my bones, tiredness warring with fear until fear was all there was. Hugging myself, wondering what was worse - the darkness or the emergence of dawn and the sound of heavy boots clomping up the steps…'Lily? Lily… Where are you?'

Like I said, I shouldn't have picked her up. Dan really hates girls like that, detests the sexual bravado, the slovenly self-satisfaction. I knew he'd be livid. And increasingly Dan's rage is more than I can bear. It drains me, leaving me limp as a rag doll, a victim, useless and helpless with no one coming to make it better, no one to take away the pain... And I can see him, that's the thing - watching and waiting, feel his temper rising, know what's coming.

"So we was at this club, yeah? And Darren says to Carla–"

Leah was smearing on lip gloss like she was going to a party or something, and I could see my leather seats were wet where she'd carelessly let my coat slip.

Get rid of her. You know what's going to happen…

By then the trickle of memories became an unstoppable flood - a creaking door, a shaft of light and a silhouette. Hands that reached down to haul me up by my hair, that ball into fists, slap and punch. The same hands that would later cajole and stroke and wipe away the tears…

But Dan and I can never be parted. It's way too late now. We've come this far, and besides he'd hunt me down. I will never be free. There was no such thing as a safe house for me back then and there isn't one now. I just have to stop his rage, not give him a reason, and keep control of things.

This stupid, vacuous girl has to go.

"Look, Leah, I need to drop you here."

Up ahead was a service station - not a great one, admittedly, with HGVs lined up outside and a flashing neon sign over a truckers' café - but a haven nonetheless.   She looked up from texting, staring through the frantic windscreen wipers into a night lashed with rain. "Oh, great."

I could picture Dan shaking his head, jaw hardening, 'She said what? Ungrateful bitch.'

"Look, I have to turn off soon anyway and at least you can get a coffee here until the rain stops."

Just go.

The Merc glided into a car park that had to be one of the saddest places on earth - petroleum laced puddles, men with beer bellies looking out through grime-smeared windows into a night they couldn't see - and left her there. A stick figure with mascara smudged eyes sticking up one single, defiant finger at my retreating lights.

Well, I'm sorry but I couldn't think about her anymore. I had to get home and fast. Foot down hard, I swung the car out across both lanes amid a cacophony of horn blowing. Dan, Dan, I'm sorry   I shouldn't have. I was so close, almost home, almost there. I glanced at the clock on the dashboard - eight-thirty. Not so bad. There was time yet, time to deal with him, to control the situation. Surely. If only I hadn't picked up that girl, slowed down, chatted... And if only it hadn't been raining.

Signs for Darlington materialised out of the gloom. The rain was easing off, giving way to chasing clouds and buffeting winds. A long, empty road and then suburbia with its neat lawns and closed curtains, ordinary people tucked up safe and warm. Our house is large and stone built, the driveway lined with cedars that bent and bounced in the gusts that shook them, ghostly shrubs quivering on the lawn, rivers of rainwater washing mushy, yellow leaves down the tarmac, bubbling out of drains and dripping from gutters.

I put my key in the lock. Turned it. And stepped into the silent, darkened hallway.

The onslaught was vicious. One of the worst. Filthy, mangled words of hatred, paintings ripped from walls, glass shattered, the release of a pent up fury that left me shaking, hands and arms covering my head, tears streaming down my face, hugging myself, rocking and pleading for it to stop.

Later, how much later I couldn't say – lost hours, days even - strung together in fitful, restless dreams – I found myself once again clutching an empty bottle of vodka, peering out from the hair strewn across my eyes. The letter box clunked and I raised my aching head. Another day, then? A grey, washed out kind of brightness. And the early papers.

The photo staring up at me from the tabloid was a bit of a jolt as I sat at the kitchen table downing cup after cup of hot coffee. Leah - a smiling schoolgirl of 15 had been a runaway. The first time she'd ever left home, both parents frantic. She'd been found badly beaten but alive somewhere off the A1 near Scotch Corner. Alive though. That was the thing.

My distorted reflection in the stainless steel fridge looked back at me with a strangely triumphant expression. I did it.

'So, Dan, you didn't get this one, did you? We got home in time. Dumped the girl before the rage set in.'

I laughed, a sound that rang hollow and hung in the air like the ghost of a child. Like Lily - the little girl covered in bruises who lives inside me. I keep all three of us tightly locked in. Only sometimes I forget how strong he is and Dan pushes aside to kill the types of girls he hates.

Leah got lucky. We really shouldn't pick them up.

THE END

Girl in the Rain was first published by: Ether books.com 2011

7. The Last Bus Home

The bus chugs home like so many times before. And Ruby, pale face staring out into the black night, is thinking about Lewis. About marrying him. About tonight and how he bought her an engagement ring and what her dad's going to say about that.

She twiddles the cheap, silver plated ring as the bus lurches to a halt and the remaining two passengers stumble down the steps, pulling their coats around them as they face the howling wind and vanish into the darkness. Ruby's stop is the last one and there are many miles to go yet. She closes her eyes and dreams of Lewis, of his lovely, golden-skinned smile as he waved her off from the bus station, the town still buzzing with lights and pumping with music. He'd probably go back to the pub for a last half, maybe onto a club. She tries to quell the rising irritation. The fact that her family has to live right out here in the wilderness, far away from town where there are jobs and people and life. Here where there is nothing but sheep and thousands of acres covered in rocks, bogs and heather. Where the last bus home is at ten o'clock. Lewis had kissed her hair and pulled her close. "Miss it," he whispered, his hands travelling down her back. "Stay with me."

The surge of response shook her. But no, not yet. Let her speak to Dad first. Dad's face. She pictures the tightening of his mouth and the torn emotions in his soft, hazel eyes. Her mother's delight, then anxious bird-like glances, waiting for Dad's response. How is she going to phrase this for the best? Lewis works as a waiter in a downtown café - there is no way she can dress that up.   Finally she sees the lights of Moor End Farm bobbing in the gloom as the bus crawls ever higher, clunking into potholes, changing down a gear, heaving forwards again. Then the white mail box at the bottom of the drive, and as always her heart lifts at the sight of home, the pull strong - reminders of school days when she and her brothers would be the only kids left on the bus, eager to charge into the farmhouse kitchen to see what was cooking - maybe a batch of scones or a hot sponge.

Ruby reaches for her bag and buttons her coat, stands and begins to make her way towards the front of the bus. There's a slight dip as it levels with the farm gates and she holds tightly onto the pole, waiting for the screeching stop. Except tonight the bus doesn't stop. He heart jumps. Suddenly there is an almighty acceleration as the mail box flies past her line of vision. "Hey! What's—"

The bus is careering into the night like a getaway vehicle at top speed, engines screaming, bouncing in and out of potholes. She crawls on her hands and knees, thrown violently from one side of the bus to the other, trying to grab onto a seat. The driver is chuckling. She hadn't noticed him when she got on with the crowd, expecting it would be old Percy, the only driver, presumably, who didn't mind spending his Saturday night chugging along the moors and back again. Only this isn't Percy.

She stares wide-eyed at the maniacal grin that turns her way. At the empty eyes and yellow tombstone teeth. There is a cold drop in the pit of her stomach. Blindly she lunges forwards to grab the steering wheel, hitting his head repeatedly with her bag. There is no plan, except nothing would be worse than being alone with this man on the moors, and at least this way there is a chance of escape. He's laughing louder and there is a wild frenzy of hair and hands until the bus suddenly hits a boulder and is thrown from the road.   For the longest time there is silence. And then a sickening crunch.

Over and over it rolls, glass smashing, metal crunching. Until finally it stops, hissing and steaming in the mud, rocks and gorse.

It is some time before Ruby, who has been thrown clear, opens her eyes. There are millions of stars in the jet sky. A fine mist scudding over a crescent moon. Her head hurts. And then she remembers. Nervously scans the area for signs of the driver. A low moan - is it the wind sweeping the moors or is it him exhaling a ghastly breath? There's no time to lose. She has to get home. Fast. Several miles have been covered and it's a long way to walk, especially with the darkness so thick it's almost palpable. She stumbles, every step an effort like walking underwater. Holding out her hands in front, she tests each footfall, forcing herself not to check over her shoulder. Was he lunging after her? Oh God, the going was so slow, so painful…*Don't look round… just keep going…*

Mist rolls over the moors as the early hours creep in, and her hair soaks up the fine drizzle, dripping darkly down her back, thin dress clinging to her skin. But she will soon be home. She has lived here all the seventeen years of her life and knows every landmark from winters helping Dad rescue sheep, to exploring the moors with her brothers on their ponies and bikes, picnics packed for the day. Here now, the stone monolith claiming 15 miles to town. She grabs it, feeling the solid familiarity beneath her half-numb and bleeding fingers. *Not long now. Keep going.*

She starts to sing. Softly at first. And then more loudly, "Early one morning, just as the sun was rising..." As if Dad will hear her and respond with his whistling, like he used to when she was had to come home alone on the school bus in the dark. She would run down the long driveway, singing at the top of her voice and Dad would come out with his lantern, whistling, waiting for her.

Ruby starts to cry.

And then - her insides skip and her heart picks up - their white mail box. She starts to run, stumbling forwards, hands stretched out ahead. She can see the mail box. It's there. Almost there. At last.

"Mum! Dad!" She's shouting now. They must be worried, maybe out looking for her. It's been hours. Every little thing is passing through her mind - the first pony, a stocky, little piebald with a mind of his own - Dad leading her round and round the field on it when he was dead on his feet from lambing all day. And Mum insisting Ruby have her own private bedroom away from her brothers, painting it herself in sunshine yellow, giving her a copy of her first ever grown-up novel - 'I Capture the Castle,' by Dodie Smith. She still has the book, read so many times the pages are tissue thin.

"Mum! Dad!"

How odd, though. The farmhouse, now that's she's here, is all darkness.

Ruby hammers on the door, rushes over to the kitchen window. *Home. Oh thank God she's home*. She peers in - no-one there. They must be out searching for her. The land rover's out.

"Let me in! Anyone! Luke! Jason!"

But the tiredness. It's like a huge weight pressing her down and down. She could sleep right here on the muddy yard. It takes the last of her energy - palms against the solid stone walls of the house, to find an open window. Scratching and scrabbling at the latch, she pushes herself through the narrow gap, landing like a slug into the gloomy house, crawls upstairs and throws herself onto the bed. *Safety. At last.*

***

Lewis sighs and puts down the phone. Another couple interested in Moor End Farm. Outsiders of course. No local wants to live there, only crazies from the cities who fancy a life far away from it all. They won't last long: if they buy it, which they probably will because of the price and the acreage, it will be a matter of months if not weeks before they leave. Very few people can live with pounding on the windows in the dead of night, doors being flung open and shouts from the dark, windswept moors. Out they stumble into the pitch blackness: "Who's there? Who's there?"

Lewis twists the cheap, silver plated ring he wears on a chain around his neck. Forty years ago now. Forty years since Ruby died at the scene of that tragic accident. Since her family moved away to try and rebuild their lives. And since he went back to college to try and rebuild his.

With thoughts of the farm once more, the air freezes and he clasps the ring tightly. "Ruby. Ah, Ruby. Don't worry, they won't stay. You'll have your home to yourself again soon…I promise."

THE END

Last Bus Home was first published by: Ether books.com 2012

8. The Midnight People

6am and bitterly cold. For most people the day would soon begin, but for those who had lain awake listening to his all-night radio show, the endlessness of grey dawn stretched ahead as usual. He called them his midnight people.

Leo pulled up his collar against the morning chill, footsteps echoing as he headed towards the neon-lit café on the corner. Open all night, the aroma of freshly percolated coffee and sizzling bacon drew in cabbies, shift workers and insomniacs alike. Okay, so Ellen thought he was crazy - always heading straight home to bed herself after the show. But for Leo it was the best part of the day - staring through the steamy windows as hot, bitter espresso woke up his taste buds; watching the light chase shadows back under doors and into offices as the world of daylight people eased into life. Tired, pillow-creased faces stared unseeingly from bus windows at their own pale reflections, and council workers swept away the night's debris, preparing for a new day.

This had been his routine for nearly a year now and it suited him just fine. "Great show last night, Leo."

Leo blinked, looked up and smiled at Dot, the café proprietor. He held out his cup while she poured in more coffee. "Thanks."

"Shame that girl didn't phone last night."

"Natasha?"

Everyone was asking about Natasha. Even the local paper had got hold of the story and some of the midnight people were blogging about her too. Nothing like a real, live on-air romance for people to gossip about.

"That's the one." Dot gave him a saucy wink. "Got a thing for you, I'd say." Leo forced another smile. As if anyone could possibly have a thing for him now - with his neck collar and more metal pins holding his limbs together than Bionic Man. Besides, with Jenny gone, his heart had a hole in it the size of a crater. Nothing left to give.

Odd though, about Natasha. He'd kind of got used to her calling the show, his pulse picking up when he heard her voice.

At 7.45 am Leo paid his bill, folded up his newspaper, and made his way to the library. Today he would read about the big bang theory. Another day it might be child psychology. Anything. As long as it took his mind off his life and everything he'd hoped it would be before the accident. Before Jenny. Eventually he would drift home, like a ghost amongst the daylight people, to what he hoped would be a deep and dreamless sleep. But rarely was.

***

Midnight: Lights. Music. Action.

"Bet she calls tonight," said Ellen, putting on her headphones.

Leo could only raise his eyebrows in

response, as the countdown for the show began: 'Three-two-one...'

Automatically his voice dropped into a molasses-thick drawl that had earned him near cult status with his listeners. "Leo here for the Leo Logan show. Time to relax, kick off your shoes and listen to some great music"

Lazy jazz oozed onto the airwaves as he took off his headphones.

"I'll fetch some coffee."

"Actually I'll bet you ten pounds she calls tonight," said Ellen.

Leo affected shock. "What? Have I got 'Gullible' stamped across my forehead? No, make it something trickier - at least what she actually requests." "Okay then - how about, 'Miss You Nights'?"

"Could be." That was certainly one of Natasha's favourites. "But I think it'll be, 'Help Me Make it Through the Night'." He tapped the side of his nose. "Call me psychic but that's the one she'll go with. And make it twenty."

"Ooh. Mr Confident."

Usually Natasha called in around 1am. If she hadn't called by 1.30am then generally speaking, she wasn't going to.

It was 1.25am when Ellen took off her specs and rubbed the bridge of her nose. "Feeling a bit tired tonight," she said.

Leo wondered why she drove herself so hard. Like all the midnight people he guessed she had her reasons, and he suspected that like him, she couldn't sleep and when she did - the dreams came in a rush like the dark wall of a car crash.

"More of that lousy coffee?"
She nodded, managing a weary smile. Their eyes met and for a moment it looked as if she was about to say something. Leo waited. But then she bent her head to rummage for a tissue and the moment dissolved.

At 1.32 am Natasha called the show. Static buzzed down the line.

"Hey, Natasha! How are you?"
After a couple of seconds Natasha said, "Hi Leo!"

He could almost hear the midnight people sigh with pleasure, fingers hovering over keyboards for the next instalment.

"Like to tell me what's keeping you awake tonight, Natasha?"

Natasha's voice was tiny and high like something Tinkerbell would have. She spoke all in a rush, "You know when there aren't any stars? When it's foggy and your house is surrounded by a thick blanket and you can't see? I get so scared sometimes."   "I know what you mean."

"I'm so alone."
"We're always here for you, Natasha."

"Do you feel lonely too, Leo?"
Leo hesitated. A line, he was sure, had been crossed. Something about the early hours made people confess secrets and dreams, but rarely did they make it personal with him in the way that Natasha did.

He sensed the listeners hold their collective breath and quickly decided not to bluff or try to lighten the mood. You always had to be careful with midnight people. "Yes," he said. "As a matter of fact I do."

Beside him Ellen stiffened.

"So, what can we play to chase away those shadows for you, Natasha? How about 'Help me Make it through–"

"That's cheating," Ellen mouthed furiously.

"I Will Always Love You,'" said Natasha. "The Dolly Parton version."

Leo looked at the two twenties he and Ellen had put on the desk and cringed inside. They had a broken-hearted girl here and the two of them had been taking bets. "I think she's in love with you," Ellen sniffed, blowing her nose.

"No, I think she's just very, very lonely."

But crawling underneath his skin and lodging there was the thought that he was her lifeline - as if there was an invisible thread between them that she was holding on to.

***

"Natasha sounded so sad last night," said Dot, putting a plate of bacon and eggs in front of him later that morning.

Leo grimaced. Just a hunch. But he too thought he'd detected a subtle change of mood, as if things might be coming to a head, or an end.

After a tormented, sleepless day, he took a stroll across the beach just as the sun was dropping like a flaming ball into the ocean. The sea hissed and shrank from the pebbles as darkness crept along the shore, lengthening his shadow. Along the coastline, lights flicked on and blinds were drawn. Soon it would be night again - alone with the midnight people, prowling foxes and the belts of grey fog that rolled in from the sea.

Arriving at work early he was surprised to find Ellen, pink eyed and pale, already there. Why did she do this? Surely a young woman like her should be out partying, not working nights with an old cynic like himself? Well, he said old - he wasn't - he just felt as old as time. She'd evaded the topic when he'd asked her once, muttering something about it being her only way into radio. But Ellen never took holidays and to his knowledge there was no boyfriend, no 'Mr Ellen'.

"Actually I don't feel too good," she admitted.

"Why don't you go home?"

The producer was counting him in: "Three-two-one..."

Leo's voice immediately dipped into honey-coated dark chocolate, "It's midnight and you know what that means. It's the Leo Logan Show. Time to relax, unwind and enjoy…"

As Sade's silky tones began to croon, 'Smooth Operator,' over the airwaves, he noticed Ellen disappearing and unexpectedly his spirits plunged. Without her it would be a long night.

At 3 am, however, Natasha called, catching

him off guard.

"Hi Leo." She started to tell him about swirling fog and hearing muffled voices. "I get so frightened. It's like I don't know where I am."

Leo struggled to understand, sensing her loneliness and wanting to help. Instead he asked her what music she'd like.

Static buzzed for a moment. Then she said, "You know that song, 'Did you happen to see the most beautiful girl…?"

They both finished the lyrics together, "And if you did…?"

"I know it," said Leo.

"Then go find her," said Natasha.

"What do you–?"

But the line was dead.

Go find her. Go find her…All night the words reverberated in his head. Whatever had she meant by that? It just got stranger.

Next morning Dot was up to the toast and marmalade stage before she broached the subject. "What do you think she meant last night about go and find her?" Leo shrugged. "I honestly don't know, Dot."

"Hmm, I think she wants you to find out who she is."

He frowned. Natasha hadn't meant that. He was almost sure.

Ellen was off sick again the next night and the next. Nobody had heard from her and it hit Leo that he'd never asked, after nearly a year of working together, whether she lived alone. He soon found out that she did. By 6am he decided to find out if she was okay. And by 6.30 a sense of urgency gripped him. When she answered the door to her flat wearing a pale pink dressing gown, her elfin face pinched and pale, something welled up from deep inside him and the urge to wrap her in his arms was overwhelming. *Go find her….Go find her…*This was it. His hollow heart flooded with warmth.

"I heard what she said the other night," Ellen croaked as she snuggled against his chest. "Do you think she meant me?" Their glances met and both smiled shyly as the early morning sun slanted through the blinds. And a new day began.

***

Natasha never called the station again, a fact remarked upon and discussed by many. A heated local debate followed. The press pushed for a campaign to find Natasha and then, as quickly as the issue arose it was dropped.

Night after night, Leo and Ellen sat listening to the debate, hands held tightly. The blinking emergence into the world of daylight people had not been easy for either of them, disquiet mellowing only with time, ghosts receding gradually and gracefully into the shadows. Moving into the glare of the sun took courage and each other, the pace of life faster, the noises sharper. Eventually Leo resumed his position at the local paper where he had worked with Jenny; and Ellen found part time work as an assistant producer with the radio station.

A year later they married. A quiet ceremony at a church near the beach. An ancient creaking building that rattled with ocean breezes and dozed to the crash of pounding surf. The day was bright and clear with scudding clouds chasing sunshine over the hills. And later, hours and hours away, after a bouncing flight through the velvet night, they arrived at a tiny Caribbean island.

Exhausted, they slept with the patio doors open, lying deeply and dreamlessly, content, still holding hands.

At 1.27 am precisely the phone rang.

Automatically Leo stretched out an arm.

Static. And then a tiny Tinkerbell voice squeaked excitedly, "It's Natasha. I'm through the fog. I found what I had to do so you could live again. And now I'm free. We both are."

Suddenly he remembered - *Natasha! It was Jenny's favourite name – she always said if they had a little girl she'd have called her Natasha! How could he have forgotten?*

"There's so much light here."

He struggled to understand. "Light? Where?"

"Good-bye, Leo. Be happy."

"No, don't go…Jenny–"

As soon as Ellen woke he related what had happened, but she started shaking her head. "No, Leo - it must have been a dream."

"But don't you see? She loved the name," Leo insisted. "It all makes sense! That was no dream - it was Jenny."

Ellen leaned over and kissed him gently. "I believe you, Leo. But look!"

She was staring at the conch by the side of the bed - this was a tiny island retreat. With no phone lines.

THE END

'Midnight Caller' was first published by:
1. My Weekly Magazine, UK. 15/01/2011
2. ether books.com 2012

9. 'Buried Too Deep': Parts 1 - 3

Part 1

1992: High Bank Farmhouse
Derbyshire.

This Halloween party was getting out of hand. Sixteen year old Megan, who had gone with her school friends, Amy and Hannah, sunk low in her corner of the sofa as the walls of the farmhouse thumped with base music and the ceiling spun like a roulette wheel. Watching Toby flirt with Amy was sickening. She picked up another bottle of cider and poured it down her throat.

Blonde, giggly Amy - in her tight jeans and off-the-shoulder sweater - had gravitated towards Toby, who was pulling her onto his knee.

Megan rose unsteadily and staggered over towards them.

"What's up with you?" he said, black eyes glinting dangerously.

Amy giggled, tightening her arms around Toby's neck.

Megan stood swaying. Why had he changed towards her? Undecided on whether to shout at him or run from the room, she looked towards the window: outside, a bank of fog had rolled across the moors, smothering everything with its thick, wet blanket. All she could see was her own ghostly reflection, alongside a couple of withered, glowing pumpkins with their cut-out grins.

"You can't go anywhere, Meg," Toby said. "Besides - I can do what I want - I don't belong to you."

'That's not,' she wanted to say, 'what you said to me yesterday, when you made love to me in the barn.' *Why was he doing this to her? Pushing her away like this? It didn't make sense.*

Tears filled her eyes at the same time as all the cider she'd sunk lurched into her throat. She bolted for the door.

At the exact moment a pair of gnarled hands suddenly slammed against the window pane, pounding frantically, and a wild-eyed, wizened face appeared from out of the gloom....

"What the…?"

The boys ran out into the farmyard - whirling round and round with torches, shouting, 'Who's there?" Balls of muggy light shone weakly in the dull, wet fog.

Meanwhile, down by the side of the house next to the kitchen, Megan was quietly and wretchedly sick. She stood gasping, wiping away her tears, swallowing acid. Waiting for all the shouting to stop. *What a horrible party. A horrible night. She should never have come here.*

Then a door slammed shut.

Night's breath rustled the tree tops.

Then came the dull plod, plod, plod of slow footsteps on the yard. She stiffened. Ears straining.

The horses in the stables were shuffling around, kicking their stalls. Something was wrong - *that face at the window*!

And then she was running. Tearing blindly down the driveway and out onto the lane, the dead sound of her own heels on concrete, her panting blacking out Toby's cruel rejection.

You can't go anywhere, Meg...

Oh no? Watch me, she thought... All she had to do was keep running.

***

Present Day: 2013
Docklands. London.

Mum had been ill for a while, but the message had still come as a shock. Megan had been working on a report about Government finances. Her head throbbed, and her neck and shoulders had welded into a shawl of steel. She pushed back her chair and ran her fingers through her long, auburn hair, thinking she must get it cut, found an elastic band in her desk top drawer and wound it into a tight little knot. She'd not been to the gym recently either - no time - not enough hours in the day.

And now her brain had ceased to work properly too - probably best to get a coffee and let her head clear. So many things to think about - Mum being ill and not being able to be there enough for her; Glen, oh dear, Glen - who'd wanted to come home with her to visit Mum, to support her like the nice guy he was...but...Oh just, but!

The phone rang. The hospice. Her mother was dead.

The bit where she grabbed her belongings, took the tube to her flat, phoned people, jumped into her car and headed out to the M1 was a blur. Was it possible for adrenaline to keep powering through your body for such a long time - for your hands to shake for hours on end? She'd reached the Chesterfield turn-off before she knew it. Had to stop. Get herself together before she arrived home.

Home. Always.

The golden oaks lining the road out to the Peaks, soon gave way to moor lands painted in a purple haze of glorious heather. She flicked open the sunroof - crisp, fresh air caressing her face; and that familiar exhilaration at the beauty of her childhood home. Only autumn produced these azure-sky days - brilliantly shot with coppery reds and burnished bronze. A kestrel hovered overhead…But nothing was the same anymore, was it?

It hit her like an express train - the pain of loss - in the stomach, the chest - her whole body convulsing with sobs - and she had to pull over.

By the time she reached the old stone hotel in Calver, with its real fire and trays of tea and scones, the afternoon was already chilling. She'd just tidy herself up, recuperate, and be on her way. What would her mother have said? *Splash your face with cold water and paint on a smile…*

The whole thing took a while. Every time she decided to apply some lipstick and continue on home, she ordered another pot of tea instead. In the end she wandered around the shops, then threw on an extra cardigan and took a walk in Chatsworth Park.

Hugging herself, head down, not a soul around - trying to find the strength she'd need - knew she'd have to provide. And by the time she reached the family cottage it was dark. No smoke from the chimney, though. Not today. Dad was waiting by the window, his face drained of life. And she fell into his arms.

But that was a week ago. Today was Mum's funeral and the whole family had arrived. She put a brave face on, hugging cousins, kissing the cheeks of frazzled great aunts she barely remembered. Handing round trays of sausage rolls, sherry and hot tea in the village hall afterwards.

Time hadn't really moved on in villages like ours, she thought, observing the matriarchal, broad-beamed older women busy with buttering bread in the tiny, back kitchen. The gossip. The hushed tones and furtive glances. Megan smiled sadly to herself, leaning against the doorway. Mum had been such a part of this tightly-woven community.

Both she and Dad had been born and raised here. Rarely left except for a holiday in Scarborough to Mum's cousin. Her own cosmopolitan life had been a source of mystery to them both - her dissertation spent in Paris, placements in New York and Toronto. They'd never even taken the train to her apartment in Docklands - seen the view of the Thames from her living room window; the glass tower she spent her days and evenings working in. Oh Mum, she thought, unable to stem the hot tears from overflowing - why didn't I visit more often?

Sometimes it had only been a few times a year - just whizzing in and out like a kind of duty call, arriving home late on a Saturday night, helping with Sunday lunch and then shooting back to London - and most of that time she'd spent on her iPhone. Her mother's frustration now echoed sadly. *Will you put that gadget away for just five minutes, Meg, and help me lay the table?*

It was shameful. Tears dripped down her face - they hadn't even had chance to discuss Glen. He'd asked her to marry him. Mum wouldn't be at the wedding - and yet it was something she'd waited so patiently for all these years, trying not to ask but desperate to, all the same. *Is this the one, Meg?*

Glen had visited for the first time a month ago, just before Mum had been hospitalised. Being a GP and a kind, gentle soul, he'd known just what to say. But her mother saw through people - knew instinctively if she could trust them - some of the village women went to her regularly for readings with tarot or tea-leaves. Megan had always laughed, said it was nonsense. Thing was though - she'd have known if Glen was right for her daughter… Only the next time Megan had visited - two weeks later - her mother was drifting in and out of consciousness, and it was a discussion they'd never had.

She tuned back in at the sound of her mother's name.

"Patsy would have known - she knew what happened afore but couldn't prove it. Oh I do miss 'er. I've known 'er all me life."

Megan dried her eyes with a tissue. That was right - these women had all been together since primary school - they knew everything about each other. Mum had been popular and enjoyed her life to the full, comfortably surrounded by friends and family. Unlike herself. So unlike herself.

Anyway, she had no right to listen in to their grief - they all missed her mum in different ways.

She was about to turn away when the conversation suddenly turned. One of the women said, "She was the only one who knew what happened to Kathleen Archer. Nobody could prove it all them years back, and now look - it's 'appened again, I'm sure of it. Patsy said as much: she said something would 'appen if that son of Rick's ever got married."

"Did her utmost to make sure Megan didn't carry on with Toby that's for sure, but then you can't stop 'em can you? At least Meg got away and did well for 'erself, bless 'er. Ooh it makes you shudder to think."

"But that lass going missing on 'er wedding night - well it's awful."

"Aye, it's shocking," the woman buttering slices of white, was saying.

Megan frowned. What was this? She didn't really want to know. But then the other woman, who was layering with ham and doing the slicing, said, "Weren't it at the reception? Apparently she just disappeared and were never seen again. I mean it's unheard of!"

Megan's reporter ears pricked up. Who only just married? Rick's son? Toby Cain?

"And did t' police find owt?"

"Well, all as I know is what were in t' papers last week ... that no actual body were found; and they had no cause for suspicion. Whatever that means when it's at 'ome. I mean - for 'er to just vanish into thin air!"

"And on top of all that what went on afore - with Kathleen - horrible place up there on t' moors."

"Like father like son. And now two women what's disappeared!"

Megan flattened herself against the wall, inching away…her heart thumping solidly against her ribs. So Toby had married. Of course he had. So why…? She closed her eyes and conjured up the image. This afternoon he'd been there at the interment, hadn't he? It was him. A dark, lean figure, shadowy among the crumbling, ivy-strewn gravestones - watching.

Distant support, her cloudy brain had reasoned. An old friend….Or maybe not. Because he did that, she remembered - watched. Way back, when she was fifteen or so… he'd watched her playing hockey one afternoon at school. A day like this - smoke in the air, crunchy leaves scattering in the wind - diverting her concentration with those sparkly, black eyes of his. Then later, out walking her dog - a curious little spaniel called Lucy - he'd been sitting on one of the drystone walls at the far end of the village. Waiting. Watching. Dark hair, black shirt, olive skin - no sign of a school uniform for him - letting Lucy nuzzle his hand.

He'd come for her then, and it looked like he'd come for her now. But why?

***

The whole thing plagued her.

She was only here, wandering around the village, she told herself, to take her mind off the grief, which had stretched from days into weeks, with Dad asking the same questions over and over - *why her and not me? Why, Meg? She didn't even smoke…I can't understand it.*

She couldn't leave him like this. Had phoned the office to say she was taking a month. Left messages with Glen, begging him not to drive up. Not yet. And the longer she stayed, the less she wanted to leave the home she'd left with an overnight bag all those years ago. Mum had been so excited when she'd won a place at university, probably never dreaming she was waving goodbye to her daughter forever.

And yet an invisible thread kept pulling her back here. This was where she needed to be so badly. Especially now.

She sat down on a bench by the river. Hands deep in her coat pockets, focusing on the icy water clambering hurriedly over the rocks.

Her mother's face. Her mother's voice.

Her mind filled with light - a late summer's day when the sun was chasing shadows across the fields - standing in the back kitchen: there had always been talk about Toby Cain and his father, and Mum hadn't liked her seeing Toby one bit, or going up to High Bank Farm. Taking on that tight-lipped, flinty eyed look she had when her daughter couldn't be controlled.

Not that Toby ever came to the house mind. He always waited on the edge of the woods where the village bordered the moors, leaning against a tree - grabbing her hand when she arrived, making her squeal. And then they'd be like wild things, chasing through the woods - taking his horses out for flat out races, lying on their backs watching kestrels or sparrow hawks. And later - when winter set in and squally, freezing rain lashed the moors sideways, saturating the peat so their feet sank and squelched with every step - later, in the barn, while the horses softly munched sweet hay.

Not that her mother could possibly have understood - or perhaps now, Megan realised, she had understood all too well.

"Something bad 'appened up there," her mother had said that afternoon. "It's a lonely place and I don't like you going."

"But what happened?" Megan had wailed.

"It were a woman as never came back, that's what," her mother said, scurrying back and forth with the washing basket. "Kathleen Archer - used to do housekeeping and whatnot - were Judy Cain's - that's Toby's mother's - best friend. Judy were never well and couldn't do all t' work. Well, Kathleen needed the money so she did the washing and that. Anyway, up she went one day and were never seen again."

"What happened to her?"

"No one knows. That's just it. She worked for 'em for a fair few year. Looking after t' little un. Toby would have been about four or maybe five year old, I suppose - same as you - when she vanished. Kathleen were up there every day. Left her own kids with her mother. I think she looked after Judy a fair bit as well. They were always close at school - you know 'ow some girls are? Like you and that Amy? Anyhow, one day she just never came back."

"Was it murder?"

"Well, I don't know if it were murder but they 'ad t' police up there. Not that they found owt." Her mother had put down the washing and was staring up at the moors, at a belt of dark rain cloud that was thundering towards them. Freshly laundered sheets blew crazily on the line. "But she 'ad family, Megan. She wouldn't o' just upped and left on 'er own. None of us believed 'im - Toby's father. Like that at school Rick were - never turning up, staring at you with them dark eyes of 'is! Anyhow, like father like son, and I don't want you going up there, do you hear me?"

Teenaged Megan had narrowed her eyes. Kathleen had probably taken the bus out of town and never come back, and with all that on her plate who could blame her? Besides - it was ancient history. Toby was nothing like his grumpy old father.

That night, she'd waited 'til dark, then

jumped onto the outhouse roof from her bedroom window, and run out to meet him, as always.

***

She shook her head now, as if to shake away the memory. The light feeling had gone, the smell and feeling of her mother with it. Flexing her toes, now numb with cold, Megan thought about Toby Cain again. Would he always be there? Etched on her subconscious mind? A longing she could never run far enough away from? On tropical beaches fringed with palms; wandering around ancient cities vibrant with life and colour - he was always, always there.

Perhaps, and it was a long shot, if his father was proved to be a murderer, like her mother had suspected, and Toby himself had followed in his father's footsteps, she would finally be free of the hold he still had over her?

Well, it was a hold, wasn't it, she reasoned - if the memory of someone tied you to the bottom of a whirlpool, never letting you free?

***

Instead of heading straight back home, she decided to take a drive, up the long pot-holed lane, which wound up to the moors. From there she could see for miles - the view of the village like that from a low aircraft - a few stone houses dotted around a centre of green. The pub car-park. The river. The day was darkening rapidly, a low mist already settling.

And before she knew it - there was the turnpike for High Bank Farm.

The house stood with its back to the wild, expanse of sodden moorland, alone and blackened from weathering. From one of the chimneys a wisp of smoke coiled into the damp, night air. The long windows dark. Watchers inside not out.

Megan pulled over. It had been twenty one years since she'd run down the track from that horrible Halloween party, with Amy's triumphant laugh tinkling in her ears.

She really ought to go home - back to work, return Glen's calls. There had been four today and he was a busy man. She must be on his mind. It wasn't fair. And yet - well, Mum always said there were no coincidences, and two missing women from one house was hardly normal, even if they were thirty years apart. A woman who didn't go home to the children she lived for? A new bride who never even stayed for her wedding night, nor returned to the family home?

And finally herself - a fully trained and experienced reporter.

Perhaps she ought to find out. Just to put her mind at rest.

***

Part 2

1992: High Bank Farmhouse Derbyshire

After everyone had rushed into the yard to find the crazy man who'd banged on the window, Toby shoved Amy off his knee.

She glared at him. "Hey! You don't have to be so rough!"

But she'd served her purpose and all too willingly, he thought, since she was supposed to be Megan's best friend. Some friend. He followed the lads who were out in the yard with torches, shouting for the mad man to come out and show himself.

"Back in! Come on - he's gone. He's just a tramp, shows himself here now and again. "

"What? You've seen him before?"

"Aye. Lots of times. Come back in - the girls are missing you!"

After they had trooped back inside and slammed the door shut behind them, he did a quick scoot around for Megan, just in time to see a vague outline of her being swallowed in the fog as she ran towards the headlights of the last bus. He stood and watched. Waited until he saw it slow and stop.

She got on.

Safe.

Probably he'd never see her again. But maybe that was for the best.

***

Present Day: High Bank Lane

Derbyshire

When the telephone beeped, Megan jumped in her seat. It was dark. How long had she been sitting here in her car? While the heather-grey mists rolled in, just watching High Bank Farm - trying to imagine living in such isolation - the rooms darkening, shadows lengthening: wondering what secrets the house held, and what those within the blackened walls, had done.

Her mobile phone flashed neon bright with Glen's name. His fifth attempt to reach her that afternoon. He must be weary after a long day in surgery, and getting worried about her too. The problem was, there was too much going on her head to have spare energy for reassuring others: the more emotional grief, the more complex the emerging mystery of the past - the less she wanted to explain or discuss it. Especially with someone who would question her thoroughly when she had no answers. Like what did the High Bank Farm disappearances have to do with herself? And why did she feel compelled to investigate when the police hadn't even opened a case?

That's exactly what Glen would ask.

And he wasn't going to stop ringing either. She picked up.

"Glen. Sorry. Sorry!"

"Thank God! I've been going out of my mind worrying."

"Why? I mean - sorry!"

"You don't have to keep saying sorry, Meg. Just a call to say you're okay would be nice.

I know how close you were to your mother and how you felt about not seeing her enough and…"

"You thought I'd sunk into depression and thrown myself off the cliffs?"

"Something like that. But you're okay?"

"Yes."

"Look, I can get this weekend off and come up. Maybe help your dad a bit?"

"No! I mean - no. Don't. I'll be back by then. I promise. I just need a few more days to sort out the headstone and things. Don't come up, Glen. Please. I'd worry about you driving when you're so tired."

"Oh."

A long pause stretched out between them.

Eventually, Glen said, "To be honest, though, Meg, I had another motive."

A light flicked on at High Bank Farm. Megan's heart thudded hard in her chest. A figure had appeared at the back door. Now walking out to the yard - towards a car!

"I've got to go, Glen. Battery's low. Look - I'll phone you tomorrow, and everything is fine, honestly. I'll see you at the weekend. Don't drive up!"

The rear lights of a truck.

Megan clicked off her phone and slid down low in her seat, her heart drumming rapidly against her ribcage.

How on earth would she explain herself if Toby saw her here? And poor Glen - but how could he ever understand?

***

Thankfully, whoever it was had driven straight past. And the night was as black as a coal face by the time she parked alongside her parents' cottage half an hour later. Inside, the front room was cold, her breath steaming on the air. Dad was asleep on the sofa, his head at an angle, hands icy to the touch.

Megan pulled a blanket over him and tiptoed towards the back kitchen in her stocking feet. But he'd heard her.

"That you, Meg?"

"Sorry, Dad. You weren't waiting up for me, were you?"

It struck her - God, he looked old. All of a sudden. Overnight. Old.

"Where were you?"

"I'll put the kettle on. Do you fancy some toast?"

He nodded. "Heating's gone off."

"No fire?"

He shook his head. All zest for life leeched from him, she thought. With Mum gone. Winter coming. His daughter going back to London soon.

Wishing she didn't have to, though. She stood in the kitchen waiting for the kettle to boil. *I don't want to go back. Not now. Not ever. My heart is breaking.*

Her father leaned against the doorway. "I said, where've you been, our Meg?"

She brushed away the tears. "Out. Thinking."

They took the hot tea and plates of toast

into the front room, and Megan switched on the small fan heater Mum used to use when she did her sewing upstairs.

"I've been looking through some of your mother's things," said her father. He indicated a box of sewing threads and remnants, cookery books and embroidered pictures. "Thought Ellen and Maud might like these - the years those girls spent sewing and knitting and sharing recipes - thought they might want 'em, unless you do?"

Megan shook her head. "I'll take them round tomorrow, shall I?"

He smiled. "I was 'oping you'd say that - can't be doing with all that fussing. I've two Victoria sponges in the cupboard going off as it is, and I don't think I can eat any more hotpots."

Megan smiled. "Dad - can I ask you something? Did you know Rick Cain when you were younger? I mean - I've been hearing about things going on up at High Bank Farm and...well, I know Mum had her suspicions about a woman called Kathleen going missing, and now it seems like someone else has vanished from up there too." She tried to laugh lightly, so he wouldn't be too concerned. "You know how nosy I am?"

Her father narrowed his eyes. "You shouldn't get into certain things, Meg."

"What things?"

"Things best kept to yourself, that's what."

"But what do you know about Kathleen? I know Mum didn't like me going up there seeing Toby, but that was years ago. Look, I wouldn't ask except for this business of him getting married and his wife disappearing."

"No, Pat didn't like you going up there. She didn't like it even when you were little, if I were shoeing one of his horses and took you up there with me."

"Wait. Rewind. You took me up there as a child?"

"Aye - you'd be before school age - about four, maybe five - you and Rick's lad - played hopscotch, marbles and stuff in t' yard. Soon as you went to school that all stopped, mind. Not that she let 'im go - Judy Cain - kept the lad back til 'e were nearly seven."

A tiny fragment of memory flittered around the edges of her mind. And then skittered away again.

"Anyhow," her father was saying. "After Kathleen disappeared, which was about that time because I can remember your mum telling me to leave you with Ellen instead - you were never allowed to go up there again. She 'ad a bad feeling about it, she said. Well, you know what she were like?"

"And Rick? Were you at school together?"

"Aye when he showed up. And if he did it were just to mess about. No, I went up there to take care of his horses, that's all. Long time ago."

"And his wife? Judy? Did you know her?"

"Your mum did. Didn't like her either. And didn't like Kath doing all her work for next to nowt. You ask a lot of questions, our Meg. Is that what you've been mithering about these past few days? Because you want to be careful - Rick and his boy - well, it's best to keep out of trouble. I don't want you getting involved."

What if Faith had unearthed the truth and been silenced?

Megan stood up, bent to kiss his cheek. " I promise I'll take care. All I'll do is go to the library and check a few facts, okay? You know what I'm like, and besides - it keeps me busy. Stops me dwelling."

"Now that," said her father. "I can understand."

***

The next day was startlingly cold and bright. A light, silvery frost had left traces of glitter on the curled, crispy leaves underfoot, and a low lying whisper of mist lay in the valley. It was quite a drive, but there was a good library in town. All she needed were a few facts. Just to settle her mind. It was the not knowing, she told herself.

With the heater on full, she set off at a pace, roaring out of the village and up onto the main road, which cut a swathe through the vivid purple moorland, as the car climbed higher and higher until finally - and suddenly on the turn of a bend - there lay below a bustling metropolis. She switched on the radio and was soon tailing work traffic into town, looking for a parking space. All she needed to know was what had reportedly happened to Kathleen Archer when she herself was still a little girl - long before she and Toby got together. And then when Toby had married - what had happened to his bride? There would be proper explanations then, instead of whispered village hearsay. It wouldn't take long. Curiosity, that's all!

Later, tapping away on the library database, her brow furrowed - okay, she thought, let's go way back, first. When Kathleen went missing it must have been around 1977 onwards.

She soon found it. The incident was reported in the local paper as missing woman, Kathleen Archer, setting off as usual on housekeeping duties to High Bank Farm, but never returning home. She'd left three young children and a devastated husband. However, Police investigations had found nothing untoward. Rick and Judy Cain had said Kathleen left the farm after cleaning all day and looking after their son, Toby. However, the bus driver, who had waited a good fifteen minutes at 5.15pm on a dark and windy evening, had finally given up. No sign of her. Nothing. Assumed, he said, that she'd stayed the night. And no, it wasn't usual.

Several days later there was a further report: someone thought they'd seen Kathleen on the coast near Scarborough - perhaps she'd taken flight and now worked in a boarding house somewhere? Again, the police had investigated, but been unable to find a woman matching the description. So no conclusion, except the obvious, by then, to everyone - that's she'd had enough of such a hard life and fled.

But those who knew Kathleen continued to speculate. There was no way Kathleen would have left those children. Something had happened.

Feeling a chill across her aching back,

Megan stretched and yawned. Lunchtime already. Not much longer. The library closed at One - but she'd yet to find out about Toby's wedding.

It was odd he'd left it so late to marry. Just a couple of years older than herself, he'd never bothered with school much and been determined to carry on running the farm. Always said he wanted a wife too, and just the very idea when he talked like that, had inflamed her teenage passion: so sure it would be herself. But shadows passed behind his eyes when she'd teased him about school. Didn't he mind that he couldn't read properly?

"While you're such a little clever clogs?" he'd said, laughing, but with eyes sparking dangerously. "You're gonna be lonely in that ivory tower of yours, Meg."

Well, it was all history now, wasn't it? He'd made his preferences clear a long time ago. But it was odd - that he hadn't married anyone in all that time. Choosing to live up there with just his bad-tempered old father for company.

Rick Cain, old before his time - occasionally rattled into the village store for supplies - his hair now tufty and grey, eyes bleary and bloodshot. 'The old reprobate', the women whispered, as he shuffled out of the co-op with a couple of carrier bags of whisky. 'Tch! Leaving his half-feral son to run what's left of that dilapidated farm '

But why? Why hadn't Toby married? Leaving it until he was nearly forty, and then his new wife walking out on him almost as soon as the wedding was over?

"Excuse me but we..."

Megan stared for a moment at the librarian. "Oh! I've been here ages, I'm so sorry."

"No - that's okay - it's just that we close in ten minutes." She indicated the gloomy afternoon outside. The bright morning had vanished and a low mist drizzled in its place.

Megan nodded, and quickly scanned more recent articles. Toby Cain had married just over a month ago. To a girl called Faith Peters. The photo showed him glowering, awkward in a suit; and the bride beaming happily in her wedding-cake dress, a tiara on her head. Blonde, pretty.

A slow drawing of the knife down her long-healed scar... prising it open....

Quickly, she drew her glance away from the photograph, from the old churchyard where her mother had recently been buried, from Toby's intense gaze into the camera...to the few words below. There had been a marquee reception up at High Bank Farm. Faith was the daughter of a Leeds contractor, who hired machinery to the farm. The newspaper wished them every happiness.

Two days later there was a fresh report of quite a different nature: following a fracas at a wedding reception, a young bride had been reported missing. Faith Peters had left the wedding party in a state of distress, but had not returned to the family home in Leeds either.

Megan flicked through ensuing articles while already pulling on her coat. Police had been called to High Bank Farm. The area cordoned off.

Land had been searched with dogs. And locals had started to talk about 'something happening all over again.'

However, there were no conclusions. No body found. Faith had simply walked out into the mist and been swallowed up, just like Kathleen Archer over thirty years previously.

***

She jumped up and hurried to the door, deep in thought. So there really was a mystery here. Mum was right, even if she hadn't known exactly why. Two women had vanished, presumed dead, and both from High Bank Farm.

Still there was more she needed to know. What about Kathleen's family, for instance? Had they, in fact, investigated further? Were they satisfied with the explanation that Kathleen had gone straight from the farm to somewhere on the coast in order to desert them? And what did the locals know about Toby's bride? Was anyone local present at the wedding, or was it family only?

Of course - she had her mother's belongings to give to Ellen and Maud. She knew where they lived in the village - had spent many childhood hours at their kitchen tables colouring-in, or learning how to play cat's cradle on the back doorstep.

Her mother's familiar scent rose again, and a butterfly memory flickered back into her mind without warning - playing hopscotch at the farm - drawing lines with a stick…then shimmied out again…

Megan closed her eyes - probably just an early memory triggered by what her dad had said. She'd call for a sandwich and then head back to the village.

Already an autumn mist had descended, and by the time she reached home, the village was shadowed in a murky gloom. Lamps had been lit and curtains drawn. The lanes were shiny wet and the air smelled of wood smoke. Towering over the village, the moors closed in - an army of darkness - and the tumbling river chuckled and babbled into the purple dusk.

Ellen and Maud lived next door to each other just three doors down from her parents' cottage, so Megan parked outside and rapped on the door. The two women appeared to be waiting. Teapot on the table. Three Royal Doulton cups and saucers, and a currant-loaf ready sliced and buttered.

"Hello, love," said Ellen. "We were wondering when you'd turn up."

***

Afterwards, she'd had to think, and think hard - and the only place she could really do that was outside. In the night air. Tramping through the woods with just her just own thoughts for company.

Briefly she stopped off home to change into wellies and a waterproof, light a fire for Dad, and tell him she'd be back soon.

"I don't like it," he'd said. "You going out in the pitch dark and thick fog! It's not safe like it used to be…"

But she'd gone anyway.

What she'd found out troubled her even more.

Why had Kathleen left those children?

"Everyone knew everything about everyone in those days," Ellen had said. "And Kathleen's youngest weren't well - that's why she wouldn't have left them. The twins had a heart problem, and 'er 'usband weren't up to much. No - all of us said there were no way Kath would have left 'em."

"What happened to the children?" Megan had asked.

A short silence while the fire crackled in the grate. Then Maud said, "The twins both passed away in their teens - weak hearts. It were an 'ereditary thing see, luv."

"And the husband? Wasn't he called Ken? I can remember him now. And the older girl was in my class - Sally?"

"Aye, that's right, luv. Little Sally. None of 'em went to your school afterwards, though. Ken were ranting that Rick had killed his wife - went mad with it, he did. And the children were taken in with their auntie over in Chesterfield."

"Went mad?"

"Aye, he were convinced Rick had murdered her. No on listens to him anymore. He lives on his own, down past the garage, that falling down place. You see 'im sometimes, drifting around, wandering over the moors…He never did get over it."

The face at the window during that fateful Halloween party?

Megan took as sip of tea, aware of both sets of beady eyes on her. An air of expectation.

"But why would Ken think Rick killed his wife? Wouldn't the police have found out if he had?"

Maud and Ellen exchanged a meaningful glance. A faint nod from Ellen and Maud continued. "Well your mum always had a feeling something weren't right up at High Bank - that there was more going on than Kath would admit to."

"Why?"

Ellen leaned forward. "Well Kathleen stopped speaking to t' rest of us. We were all such good friends right from schooldays, well, all apart from Judy - Rick's wife - what a piece of work she was!

"Then Kath went to work for Judy up at High Bank, and suddenly she'd cut you in the street. We reckon, and it's only guesswork mind, that something were going on she didn't want the rest of us to know about. Something she might have told Ken - 'er 'usband."

Megan's brow furrowed deeply. "Something illegal? Some sort of secret she had to keep?"

Maud picked up her tea cup. "Your mum never liked Judy Cain. Said she were using Kathleen to do all her dirty work for her. Lying in bed like Lady Muck. Now why would Kath put up with all that? Do you see where I'm going, luv?"

Megan shook her foggy brain but it wouldn't clear. "Judy had something on Kathleen, you mean?"

Ellen raised her eyebrows. "Maybe. And Ken knew about it. For t' rest of us it's still a mystery as to what it were."

"But for some reason Ken either hasn't told the police or it didn't cut any ice - no solid evidence of whatever it was, perhaps? It could have been an accident, though, couldn't it? After some kind of argument? But no body, that's the thing! The police didn't find a body." Her voice trailed off.

Maud started to clear away the china cups, and Megan realised it was her cue to leave. The old ladies had said all they had to say and the rest would be pure speculation.

Parting with promises not to leave it so long next time, and with a lemon drizzle cake tucked into a tin for her dad, Megan had left and dashed immediately home.

Walking through the dripping woods, breathing in the Autumnal air of wet leaves and damp earth, her thoughts finally cleared to reveal a single path. A path which led to a locked and bolted door. Toby's. Whatever it was - he knew! He'd wanted rid of her all those years ago, hadn't he? No explanation, and about as blunt as a mallet - just, now she came to think of it - after he'd started talking about how they'd marry one day - that rainy day they'd spent in the barn and made love for the first and last time.

Now it seemed his wife, Faith, had found

something out! Something which stemmed back to the night Kathleen disappeared.

Her heart picked up several beats.

Could she, though? See him again? And would that put herself at risk?

Well she had to. And tonight too. Because time was running out and probably she'd never get another chance.

She made a sudden about turn. Tracking homewards.

As she did so, a shadowy figure darted quickly behind the trees. A man.   Megan stood still. Held her breath. No - nothing. She began to walk fast. Was it Toby watching her again? Did he know she'd been asking questions? Boy, he really must have something to hide.

The village lights bobbed up and down on the edge of her vision as she picked up speed. Oh this was silly. It was just someone out for a solitary walk like herself. Didn't want to be seen, that's all . *It's not safe like it used to be.*

When she reached the gate to the back garden, Megan turned and scanned the field down as far as the woods. Nothing. No one.

She was being ridiculous.

***

All the same - the sooner she got to the bottom of this the better. Wrapped it up as they said at work.

Back home, Dad had turned on the television and made a pot of tea. "Glen called," he said.

"What did he say?"

"That your phone was off. He was wanting to come up - said he'd something to tell you."

"I'll ring him when I get back."

"Why? Where are you going now? "

Ignoring his question, she kissed the top of his head. "You seem brighter?"

He did. His cheeks had colour and the remains of a meal lay on a plate beside him. "Aye. Funny thing. You know I were sorting out some of your mother's things? Well I found those daft cards of hers, and I got this feeling - like I could smell her rose talc and the Shalimar I used to get 'er. I think she' still with me, Meg. Does that sound daft?"

"No." She gave him a hug. "I think she's with me too. That's why you needn't worry. Anyway, I'm only going to see an old friend for a chat," she said, as evasive as her teenaged self had ever been. Some things never change, she thought, turning on the ignition - trying to protect our parents from the awful truth of what we really get up to when they aren't watching.

Like going to see Toby Cain.

***

Part 3

Present Day: Derbyshire

At the edge of the village, Megan took the sharp

left turn onto High Bank Lane, telling herself this was the right thing to do. She was possibly the one person who could find out what had happened to the two missing women at High Bank Farm. Her stomach churned. What had Toby's new wife, Faith, found out? Had she got too close to the truth? And had Toby really killed her because of it?

One thing was for sure - if she didn't find out now, then this would haunt her for the rest of her days. And she would never be free.

The pot-holed road was steep, and the car pitched and rolled as it lurched from one to the other, drizzly rain spotting her windscreen. With a couple of miles still to go, the car wound steadily upwards. So easy to forget, after all the years of living in a city, how remote this place was.

The solid wall of fog came as a surprise - the car instantly swallowed by it, headlights illuminating nothing but swirling grey mist.

Megan slowed right down to crawling pace until the lane finally levelled at the top. Unable to see anything at all, she parked on the verge, deciding to walk the rest of the way. Ten minutes at most. Besides - best if he didn't see her coming and have time to prepare.

Grabbing a jacket from the back seat, she stepped into the chill of the night air and locked the car behind her. The fog lay heavy and wet, her footsteps clicking on the tarmac as she walked towards the farm.

Ahead, a single lamp glowed from an upstairs window. Guiding her way. As it lay waiting in silent darkness, for her arrival.

***

Toby watched her approach from an upstairs window. Put his father's meal tray down on the ledge. Surely not? Was that Megan?

The bank of fog, which had previously engulfed the house, had rolled forwards, leaving a brief pocket of midnight sky dotted with stars. Stray wisps skirted across the moon.

Megan…twenty years ago…waiting hours and hours in the rain until his clothes were drenched - at the edge of the woods - watching for her bedroom light to flick off, for the bobbing of her torch across the fields…holding her warm body so close to his chest, fastening his arms around her …well, well…Megan Bailey! If you must dice with death…

***

The back door to the kitchen was open wide. Megan walked in. God it hadn't changed in all these years! The old range still pulsing heat. The worn flagstone floor. The slow tick-tock of an old grandfather clock in the hallway; a feeling of time standing still…

"Hello Meg!"

She swung round. Toby sitting in the dark with his back to the kitchen window. He kicked the door shut and shot the bolts across.

Her voice, she realised, was stuck

somewhere in her chest like a fruit stone, and her next breath wouldn't come.

"Looking for me?"

Ghostly moonlight silhouetted his shape, as her eyes adjusted to the darkness; and fear quivered up and down her spine. Oh, why didn't she tell Dad where she was going? How come she thought Toby would soften just for her? Tell her everything just because once, a long time ago, he'd loved her?

Finally her lungs opened and she took a deep breath. "Actually, yes."

"Never thought I'd see you again!'

"Can I sit down?"

He indicated the kitchen table and chairs. "Be my guest."

"I came home for Mum's funeral. Saw you there.'

The silence hung heavily between them.

"You should have spoken," she said, her voice sounding annoyingly timid. She cleared her throat and tried again. Stronger this time. "So why were you there? And in the woods again this afternoon?"

"You women don't know when to let it go, do you?"

"What do you mean?"

His dark, glittering eyes bored into hers.
Keep him talking…keep control…

"I heard you got married, by the way? Congratulations!"

His unrelenting stare continued to hold hers for what felt like all eternity. Eventually he said,

"You're asking a lot of questions, Meg."

"So how about answering some of them? Long time no see, Toby. I thought we'd have a catch-up."

He moved closer to her on his chair, scraping it along the flagstones. "Well not before time, eh? Why don't we open a bottle of something? To er…celebrate?"

Close up, his dark eyes were every bit as mesmerising as they'd ever been - etched now with bitterness; his long, soft mouth hardened to razor wire. He'd always been lanky, hungry looking, she recalled - and that hadn't changed: the man was sinewy and sprung tight as a coil. In spite of the gnawing, twisting fear inside, her whole being melted in response to the closeness of him. The rawness. The danger. And she smiled slightly. "Yes - that would be nice."

***

She looked around as he poured out the wine, remembering with vivid clarity the night of the party, that face appearing at the window, making them all scream out with shock.

"Elderberry," said Toby, handing her a glass of home-made brew the colour of dark cassis. "Pure nectar."

They each swallowed.

He poured more.

"So. Where is this new wife of yours, Toby?" Megan blurted out. "I mean - I don't get it - I heard you only married a few weeks ago…You must know what people are saying?"

He shrugged. "She went to Spain on our honeymoon and never came back. We had a row - you know how it is?"

She drained her second glass - the wine was indeed, nectar - and held it out for more. "No, Toby, I don't. In fact - I don't know anyone whose marriage only lasted a few hours. What happened? Seriously?"

"Made a mistake, didn't I? Convinced my...."

"Convinced? Convinced who?"

"Doesn't matter. Anyway, I thought she'd be happy here. But it seemed she just wanted to use me. Build holiday cottages and make a fortune and then sell it all on. Put my old dad in a home. Tells me this - starts gushing about all the plans she had in mind - at the wedding reception. I suppose we'd all had too much to drink and when I said, 'No. Never. Not ever - she knew what she was marrying into and what the terms were;' she flew into a rage...Started screaming at me."

"And that's when you killed her?"

His eyes widened. "Eh? No, of course I didn't kill her, you daft bat. That's what those gossiping idiots in the village are saying, I suppose, and why they called the cops on us. Again.' He shook his head in disbelief and filled their glasses again. 'I thought you of all people, knew me better than that!"

Megan hung her head.

"She took off with the honeymoon tickets, okay? Said I knew where to find her if I ever came to my senses. But no way was she going to live out here in this 'God-forsaken place' taking care of, 'my disgusting drunkard of a father.' If you don't believe me you can check my emails. She's going for annulment."

Megan nodded, her head muzzier by the minute. "And you two didn't discuss any of this beforehand?"

He laughed softly and poured them both a third glass. "Do you know, Meg, we didn't. We met cos her dad hired us machinery and she came with him once or twice. I thought she just wanted to be with me. We had a laugh - went out a few times - one thing led to another and I dared to dream. But then it turned out she'd been making plans and working it all out - thought I suppose, that once we were married I'd do what she wanted. So no - we never discussed it. Both of us assumed…And it was the first time she'd seen Dad…"

"Ah. At the reception? Was he drunk?"

"Very. And shouting. There was only me and dad from our side. About thirty-odd from hers."

He scraped back his chair. Indicated the deteriorating weather outside. A squall of rain lashed the window pane, the November night wet and cold. Wood smoke permeated the room from the downdraft, and Megan huddled into her jacket. 'So cold in here.'

He turned up the heat on the range. Uncorked another bottle.

"Looks like you'd better stay over," he said.

You can't go anywhere, Meg...

"It's a rough night and besides, you can't drive after half a bottle of this stuff!"

He sat close to her again. The scent of him. Warm. Musky.

A question skirted around in her mind - something she suddenly wanted to ask… but what was it?

"Of course you ran off, last time," he was saying, and his voice seemed so far away.

Her mind swung back to the night of the party. That horrible memory she could never erase. She laughed without mirth. "And why do you think that was?"

"Couldn't get rid of you, could I?"

She downed her fourth glass of evil brew to numb the surge of pain, as the knife drew down her scar once more. "Get rid of me?"

But his eyes were telling such a different story. Those bewitching gypsy eyes…as he leaned towards her.

Slowly, oh so slowly, their cheeks touched, his breath on hers, his lips brushing the corner of her mouth…

Then abruptly he stood up. His chair flew back along the flagstones. "You can have the spare room. I'll just get some blankets."

***

Hours later, Megan lay in total darkness listening to the sough of the wind in the trees, the creaking of the old house. Trying to get warm under a pile of musty blankets. She'd be out of here at first light. As soon as her head had stopped spinning. Oh what an idiot to drink all that wine and box herself in like this. But it had given her the courage she needed and loosened his tongue too… although there were things he'd told her that simply did not add up…

What he said about Faith wanting the two of them to find an easier path in life by turning the barns into holiday cottages - that all made perfect sense and why wouldn't she suggest her exciting plans to her new husband? Why would he so violently object to them? Of course Faith couldn't be expected to nurse his drunken father. What was wrong with wanting him to be properly cared for?

Life was hard up here and it sounded like Faith was a city girl used to having nice things. She'd fallen for Toby. Why not? He was still an extremely attractive man.

Again that clutch of rising emotion. The trace of blade against wound…

She fought against her own emotions, trying to untangle the tentacles coiling around her rational mind. *Think, just think….*

Drifting in and out of consciousness. Waking briefly. Cold. So cold. A noise. What was it? Nothing. Just the wind shaking the window panes, buffeting the walls….

Sleep dragged her down once more. Into a swirling abyss of blackness and unanswered questions. Her mother's rose-talc filled the air…and suddenly there, in a pool of light, she saw herself and Toby as children - playing in the dirt yard with sticks and marbles...

She sat shock upright.

In the dirt...

Now concrete.

A holiday cottage business... would mean digging up the barns and the yard for foundations...of course!

And there it was again. A shout. Someone really was shouting.

Megan struggled from under the blankets and out of bed. Threw a cardigan on and crept across the room. A thin sliver of ghostly moonlight lit her way. She inched open the door and began to creep down the corridor in the direction of the raised voices.

A door slammed shut, and she darted into the nearest bedroom. Footsteps coming nearer.. She shivered violently, teeth chattering, letting her eyes adjust to the gloom. And as they did so - her heart jack-hammered into her ribs, and she gasped out loud. The room was a shrine.

A white dressing table adorned with bottles of scent and hair brushes. Cushions on a white, tasselled bedspread. An ancient wooden wardrobe with one of the doors not properly shut, so that an arm of a flowery dress poked through. Wind whistled down the chimney, drawing her attention to the fireplace - and the mantelpiece peppered with china figurines.

This must have been Toby's mother's room? But why keep it like this? Oh it was creepy. The poor woman must have died of shock -

imagine your own husband killing your best friend and then burying the body under your back yard? Perhaps he killed her too?

Megan's hand flew to her mouth to stop herself from screaming out loud. Is that what Toby was covering up? And yet he cared for this father, attending to his shouts in the night... That didn't make sense, did it? How could a drunken, broken man keep such a hold on his son?

Her mind began to furiously slot the pieces into place... so much so that she never saw the door silently swing open. Revealing Toby's silhouette.

"I'm sorry,' she stammered. 'I heard voices and then I panicked, and ended up in here by mistake. I'm sorry. I can see this is your late mother's room and I didn't mean to pry."

His dark form moved towards her.

"She's not dead, Megan," he said, "in fact Mum's very much alive and well thank you. I don't know why you think there's such a trail of bodies up here."

She willed her heart to stop thumping so hard. "Alive?"

"Shall I take you back to your own room now?"

"Toby - look I heard the shouts. Why don't you get help for your dad?" She mustn't push him too far. For some unknown reason he felt duty bound to protect his father, even at the expense of his own life.

In fact, she realised, as he led her back down the corridor to her room at the end - he was every bit as tied to the past as she was. It just didn't make sense that he would be so dutiful to his murdering father. So what if Kathleen's body was found? That would be a good thing for her family, wouldn't it? And Rick would pay the price not Toby. Toby had been five years old at the time, for goodness sake.

They levelled with the doorway to her room. But there was an unknown factor here - how would Toby react if she put this to him?

She took the chance. Because she'd never get another one. Because the question burst out of her. "Toby - why don't you just leave this place? You can't be happy? And your dad clearly needs a lot of care."

"If I tell you I'd have to kill you," He laughed - a light, silvery laugh that sounded close to despair.

"But what sort of life is this?" She persisted. "I've been all over the world, whereas you…"

"Mocking me again, Meg?"

"No - of course not."

"You always thought you were better than me, didn't you?"

"What? No. Is that why you wanted to get rid of me? Because you thought that? So you flirted with Amy to make me go?"

He said nothing.

'You hurt me, Toby. Badly. Why do you think I kept running and never came home, even when I was desperate to? Even when my mother was dying?'

He still said nothing and the chasm between them deepened further.

Tearfully now she raised her voice. "And you still haven't answered my question - why were you at Mum's funeral? Answer me! What's going on?"

He held her arms with an iron grip. "Listen to me. I can't leave because I can never leave. I was at the funeral watching out for you. I always watch out for you because of Ken. Remember the face at the window that night - at the Halloween party?"

She nodded. "Who could forget?"

"Well Kathleen Archer was my mum's best friend and she died. Ken's her husband and he's been haunting us for thirty years now. I had to get rid of you because he was always here - threatening to hurt those we loved in return! It was all to protect you.'

'He thinks your dad killed Kathleen, then? His wife?'

'My dad loved Kathleen. Of course he didn't kill her.'

'What then? I don't understand - who are you protecting?'

'My mother.'

'What?'

He continued to hold her tightly. "Megan - my dad loved Kathleen! My mother had been using her to do all the hard work. Dad fell in love with Kathleen and Mum found out. Pushed her down the cellar steps, and Kathleen died."

Megan swayed. Blinked. "Where is your

mother now?"

"She's living her life. Comes back here sometimes - just to check we're holding our tongues. So as long as no one comes round here asking questions, or finds the body it will be fine."

"Not for Ken. Or his oldest daughter, Sally. Or you! Toby, you were five - why should you keep her nasty secret? She lives a full life while you and your dad protect her with yours! She's a bully, Toby. Why are you so frightened of her? You can be free!"

Toby shook his head. "Megan don't do this! You have no idea."

She smiled encouragingly. "Toby! Come on - don't you see? You have to let this come out. It's for the best. I'll help you."

"No."

"Your dad will be cared for properly. You will be free. Your mother did it and…"

"No Megan. It will kill her - she's fragile."

"No she's not. She's played you all - had another woman doing all her work pretending to be too frail. Then when your dad fell in love with poor Kathleen, she killed her. Destroyed a family. Sent the husband mad. Ruined her own husband's life, didn't send her son to school, wouldn't let him marry - and all to protect herself! Can't you see?"

Real panic skittered behind his eyes. Good God, Megan thought, no he can't - he's too entrenched and has been since he was a small child."

'No,' said Toby, moving towards her. "I won't let you."

But she took a chance and broke free, tearing down the stairs in her bare feet… a teenager in flight all over again…

His footsteps thundered after her.

'No,' he shouted. 'Don't…'

They were half way down the stairs when headlights caught them. Lighting up the stairway through the hall window. A blue light flashing against the wall. The sound of a cars, footsteps, doors slamming...

Glen must have driven up, and Dad had guessed where she was…

She swung round. "Toby - you were five! This will set you free. Trust me. Please."

Tears glistened along his dark lashes. Before her eyes he seemed to crumple like a rag doll…all those years holding his mother's secret…

As he reached out to her she held him. For the last time.

Felt his grip on her loosen.

And just like that, in an instant, it was over.

***

London. Docklands.

It took a while. Months. A long, icy winter, which swept up the Thames and froze the city with glistening white snow flurries, and a cutting wind that blew under doors and rattled windows.

But early in the following year, Megan started to pack. Folding up her previous life into suitcases and boxes. A low winter sun hung over the Thames, the London hum of industry turning over a new day. But she was going home.

Glen was on the phone in the other room, sorting out their accommodation until they found a house they both liked. He'd found a practice near Matlock - in a quiet, rural village - the news he'd been dying to tell her.

'But was it what she wanted?' he'd asked her, as they sat in his car on that early November morning outside High Bank. Did she want him? Or this Toby? Her dad had filled him in - told him of her obsession.

Megan had hung her head, not looking up as Toby was led to a police car. "I think I need a little time," she'd said.

Glen had started up the engine and driven her silently home, where she crawled into bed and stayed. By the time she emerged, it had been the following evening, to find Dad and Glen playing chess by the crackling fire. The smell of something roasting in the oven.

"The sleeper awakes," said Glen.

They smiled into each other's eyes. The feeling, she thought later, was like flailing around in water - like having surfaced after many moons submerged - and she stood blinking in the tiny living room. Here was a kind man. A man who loved her, who had taken the time to understand, forgive, and work it through. A rare soul indeed. And for the first time since she was sixteen, her heart stirred in its cage, and fluttered into life.

That had been a month ago now. Toby had been released, and according to her father, found his wife and moved to Leeds to be with her. Rick Cain had been re-housed and was being treated for alcohol addiction; and Judy arrested for the murder of Kathleen Archer more than thirty years before.

It would be a long time, Megan thought, before High Bank Farm would ever be put onto the market, now everyone knew what had happened up there. Should it ever sell, of course.

She wondered about that. About who might choose to live within those blackened, wind-blasted walls, which echoed with the ghosts of madness and deceit. Or was that just the soughing of the trees?

The End

First published in Woman's Weekly 2013

10. Headache

I always believed that when we die, that's it. Finished. Kaput. The end of our tiny, inconsequential lives. Until I met Imelda.

Imelda was a temp at the office and I was one of the reps. We sold medical equipment - catheters and scopes - and occasionally I popped in to have a word with Guy, our sales manager. Only this particular morning, instead of Ruth, our regular rottweiler in a twin-set, I was met by a willowy blonde in a mini-skirt. Not what you'd call pretty exactly - her dancing green eyes were a little too deeply set and her nose a tad too long for that, but she was certainly arresting.

"You must be Alice? Ruth's off today so I'm afraid you've got me." She held out her hand and smiled - dazzlingly unexpected. "You've got some new scopes over there," she said, pointing to a stack of heavy looking black cases. "There's one for each of you. Carol and Tina are coming in later."

Of course, they were. Carol and Tina would have arranged that purposefully so they could have Guy to themselves. Vying for top jobs sharpens knives and Guy, being a straight kind of bloke, had simply told it like it was - that I was top in sales and first in line for his position when he gained promotion. Cue the end of two friendships and hello to professional isolation. I was unhappy, of course I was, and the unhappier I became the harder I worked, and the harder I worked the more my shoulders, neck and head ached.

"Ooh, careful," said Imelda as I bent over to pick up my case, wincing with the pain that shot up my neck.

I smiled, the kind of smile you see on ballerinas faces when their shoes are too tight. I had some painkillers in the car and I didn't want to linger. I rarely stuck around for chats - running onto the next mission then the next, collapsing when I got home with a pounding headache. But Imelda seemed nice and it certainly made a change not to be glared at by Ruth or whispered about by the other girls.

"Don't worry," I said. "It's just stiffness from driving. I ought to see the doctor, but, you know–"

"Oh, it's not that," she said. "You're carrying around your dead brother's spirit around with you - that's what's doing it."

She stated this fact about as casually as if she'd said my shoes were rather nice, and I stared at her open mouthed. Well, it's not what you expect in everyday conversation, is it?

Imelda laughed - a real head-thrown-back, belly laugh. "Your face!"   I laughed too. Oops. I'd been had. Too tired to spot a bit of a leg-pull.

"Come and have a cup of tea in the kitchen. I've just put the kettle on and Guy's out until lunchtime. We can get to know each other."

I hesitated.

But evidently she wasn't taking no for an

answer. "I've got some aspirin in my desk. I'll go get them."

Well, before I knew it she was telling me everything I kind of knew already but somehow didn't - that Carol and Tina regularly popped in to see Guy, always managing to tell him how uptight, stressed out and over-ambitious *I* was. They said I was running from business call to business call, working late into the night, didn't know how to relax and had *no people skills...*

Imelda was on overdrive and I had to stop her.

"Sorry. It all sort of rushes out of me. The thing is, you're running away from yourself, from your own shadow."

"I've always been like that."

"Alice - you need to speak to your mother and soon because this spirit is catching up with you. You can't run away forever. He's part of you. And he won't rest."

"Um...speak to my mother?" *About a brother I never had*? Was she crazy?

Imelda nodded. "So, didn't you know you had a brother, then?"

"I don't. I'm sorry, Imelda. I have two younger sisters and that's it." Imelda looked back at me with a deeply unsettling gaze, and said. "But he's here, Alice, I can see him. He's called Frank. Ask your mother about him." And then she was gone, leaving me in the empty kitchen with the blinds flapping and the fluorescent lights flickering overhead.

It shouldn't have but it did. The whole

thing bugged me. So much so that when it got to the weekend I just had to bring it up with Mum. We were alone in the kitchen after Sunday lunch. She was washing and I was drying. I took a deep breath.

"Mum, er, um, look I don't know how to say this but…did I ever have a brother?"

My mother's response was to drop a plate. The crash shattered the air between us and I watched horrified as her bleeding fingers scrambled around amid shards of china still glistening with soapsuds. "How could you, Alice? For goodness sake."   "I'm sorry. It's just that this girl at work said I had a dead spirit hanging around me, and that he was causing my neck pain."

My mother glared at me through flinty eyes. "For neck pain, Alice, you see a doctor."

So I saw a doctor. In fact, during the following weeks I saw a physiotherapist, a masseuse, a chiropractor, an acupuncturist and an osteopath. But the pain racked up and was worsening by the day. Soon I could barely leave my flat without taking a cocktail of painkillers. Yet the pain increased until I could barely see. And maybe it was my imagination, but as my temples throbbed and an imaginary axe sunk into my cranium, I could have sworn my shadow was becoming longer. And darker.   People began to back away when I spoke - focusing on something slightly beyond me instead of on my eyes. And when I lay in bed at night, my fuddled brain played tricks on me - black shapes sliding around the walls and heavy breathing in my ears. I'd sit bolt upright, panting, afraid someone was in the room.

"I think you need anti-depressants," said the doctor. "And I'll refer you for a cat-scan."

So he thought it was a brain tumour, did he? I wondered what he'd say to the theory of it being a long-deceased brother I never had, clinging to my back? Nobody believes in stuff like that. Everyone would say I was crackers, losing the plot, having a breakdown, as gaga as Lady Gaga. I think at that point I began to lose all hope of ever being cured. I could just imagine the gloating when Carol and Tina heard I'd been signed off for stress and depression...

"Two months off!" Imelda gasped on the other end of the phone.

"I know. But what can I do? I can barely function."

"Frank's getting angrier, Alice. He doesn't like it that his own mother denied his existence, you know?"

"Imelda, I can't ask her again. She was livid."

"You must. Or, how can I put this? If you don't you will *never* be well."

Her words were like a punch to the gut. Nausea clogged in my throat as my shaking fingers ended the call. This could not be happening. Okay, so Imelda had some kind of psychic powers, I could accept that. After all - just because we can't see something it doesn't mean it isn't there. But this whole thing was sorely testing my rational mind. There was really only one thing I could do at that point, I thought, and that was to disprove it and put Imelda's ridiculous imaginings to bed once and for all.

On the drive over to my mother's the pain was blinding and I had to pull over several times. I took the maximum amount of analgesics advisable and drove with blurred vision.

"You look awful." said my mother, opening the door.

"So do you."

"Well, I've had a few sleepless nights. Nightmares." As she stood back to let me in, she rubbed her eyes repeatedly, and I noticed how utterly drained she looked - grey skin tone, unwashed hair. Not like her at all – not one bit.

I followed her into the kitchen and waited while she put the kettle on and spooned coffee into two mugs. She plonked the hot drinks on the table and we sat facing each other through coils of steam.

"Mum?"

She winced. Knew what was coming, I expect.

"Mum, you have to tell me. Just answer me. Please. Did I ever have a brother?"

She glared at me. Then, slowly, her lips began to tremble and her eyes filled with tears. Finally she nodded. "You had a twin. He was born just minutes after you but–" She stopped and I reached over to take her hand while the impact of what she was telling me sunk in. "There was something not right - he was very tiny. He didn't survive more than a couple of hours. We called him Frank."

Frank!

Immediately she caught the look on my face and pulled back. "I'm sorry, Alice. I know I should have told you, but there never seemed to be a right time and in the end poor Frank was just one of those things we had to put behind us."

The previously sunny kitchen flickered into darkness and we both gasped.

Frank is angry - he can't understand why you're denying him.

"Mum, Imelda says we have to acknowledge him. It's the only way."

"Alice - who on earth is this woman?"

After I described her, Mum shuddered and said, "She sounds a lot like the Imelda I knew as a little girl - your gran's sister. She died of polio when I was in my teens, though. How odd."

We talked and talked and as we did the atmosphere lightened and gradually I became aware of the pain inside my head lifting. We parted on happier terms than we had in months and as I headed out to my car an hour later, I realised something - my neck and head pain had completely gone.

At first I couldn't quite believe it. I danced around a bit, doing a little jig. Imelda had been right. All we had to do was acknowledge poor little Frank. Because here I was - free of pain at last. Oh, the joy!

The next morning I rang the office to tell Imelda the good news. In fact, I planned to take her out for a meal - anywhere she wanted.

Ruth answered. "Imelda who?" she snapped. "Never heard of her."

"Imelda. You know, the temp while you were off? Blonde hair, mini skirt?" "I haven't been off."

"But she made me tea in the kitchen–" My words trailed away as understanding crept in. Imelda had appeared at my side out of nowhere that day, and since then I'd only ever spoken to her on the phone. My skin chilled as if I'd stepped inside a tomb.

Only Ruth's voice, shrieking out of the handset, brought me out of my shocked silence. "So did you want something, only I am rather busy?"

About to say I was coming back to work I suddenly found myself saying something else entirely. I told Ruth I was handing in my notice. Risky, yes, but in my euphoria I was pretty sure I'd find a happier place in which to work. I could do anything - I was at the top of my game. In fact, imagining Ruth's face - like the rear end of a turkey – I almost giggled.

Later, still thinking about Imelda, I sauntered out to the car, swinging my briefcase in the sun, twirling my keys. Good-bye, Frank, my baby brother - gone to a higher place. Rest in peace, little one. No more headaches, no more running. No more long shadows. I twirled around - and then the smile died on my face.

The pain in my head was so sudden and so violent I crashed to the floor, vaguely aware of someone tall and blonde, walking calmly towards me through a fine mist as if she had all the time in the world. No mini-skirt this time though, just a long brown coat and a gentle smile.

"Hello again, Alice."

Oh, I didn't meet an untimely end if that's what you're thinking. No. I woke up. I could hear them talking first of all, saying how if only I'd gone for the cat scan they would have known about the aneurysm. And then how odd it was that the ambulance arrived so quickly when there was no on there but me - unconscious and lying on the floor.

Gradually their woozy faces came into focus and I realised I was coming round from an anaesthetic.

"You're going to be fine, Alice," someone said. "You must have a guardian angel."

I still see Imelda from time to time - today she was behind the bar at the local pub lecturing me about drinking too much white wine after work. Another time she'll be in a bus queue or passing by on an escalator. A quick glance of flashing green eyes and an impish grin and my heart will jump. My guardian angel? A spirit who decided to stay on after the job was done? I don't know. But I do know this - I'm quite happy to wait a very long time to find out.

THE END

<u>Headache was first published by:</u> 1. That's

Life Fast Fiction, Australia, September 2009.
Ether books.com 2012

11. A Second Opinion

Two weeks after Marlene's cremation I found her sitting on the sofa. I'd just walked into the lounge and almost dropped my tea.

"Oh for goodness sake, Geoffrey," said Julia, diving for the carpet with a wad of kitchen roll. "You're getting so clumsy in your old age."

I looked again at the sofa. That could not be Marlene. She couldn't be sitting right here in my house. It wasn't possible. And yet she was. I swear. As shockingly real to me then as she had ever been, smiling wanly as she faded into the upholstery. "Well I expect it will come out eventually," Julia was saying. "I've still got some of that carpet cleaning stuff we–" She looked over at the sofa then back at me. "What? What is it?"

"Nothing. Trick of the light, I expect. Thought I saw something."

The woman I murdered.

It had been, I quickly reassured myself, a stab of inconvenient morality. A memory, which in time would fade. *Get a grip old boy! It's done with.* Yet my age-spotted hands shook badly as I lifted the teacup to my lips. And my heart jittered about in its increasingly brittle cage. What an old fool I'd been; albeit one with an important career. But in the end - still a fool.

It was Saturday morning - papers,

breakfast, and Radio 4. A low autumn sun bathed the room, dust motes twirling, settling on us an air of timeless golden contentment. Children grown and gone. All those years stretching ahead of us. Just as it should have been. And so nearly was.

Marlene, I thought, staring for so long at the same paragraph in The Guardian that it blurred...*This should have been over.*

***

We'd met during an angioplasty: a routine procedure that saw Marlene, the anaesthetist, switch from boredom to panic in less time than it took for me to nick a major artery. The man died and the case went to court.

We consoled each other over a few shots of single malt in her flat overlooking the river. Rushing, giggling water. Crisp, white sheets. Plunging oblivion...

On the day of her funeral three months later I had a full operating list, beginning with a quadruple bypass graft and not finishing until well after her coffin had been lowered into the furnace.

"You're sweating a bit today, Sir," said my Senior Reg.

Inside the latex gloves tiny globules of guilt rolled into the crinkled wrists. God, it was hot that day. Hot as a furnace. And with wobbling, clammy fingers it was damned near impossible to thread the sutures with visions bulleting through my head - of flames leaping gleefully into auburn curls; racing across alabaster skin that melted, popped and dripped…That stench, I told myself, it was just cauterization - our own cauterizing procedure here in theatre, that was filling the air with the sickening stench of burning human flesh, not–

"Are you all right, Sir?"

"Bit below par, Anderson. Might grab an early lunch."

The graft had been a success, but it was best I thought, to leave the rest of the list to him. 'Flu,' I muttered, hurrying out. Something like that.

And half an hour later I was sitting outside the little pub by the canal she and I used to frequent. One particular day replayed inside my head: Marlene sitting with her face to the sun while I talked about a clinical paper and a trip to Tokyo to present it. Maybe she would like to come?

She'd smiled and reached across the table. "Oh Geoff, I've never felt so happy. Ecstatic. I feel like running barefoot through the grass, or wading up to my thighs in the river, or making love in the bluebells. I feel alive, Geoff. For the first time ever!"

Her voice was loud and people were looking.

I pulled back my hands. "Right. Well, um, must get back to work - clinic this afternoon, old girl."

"Why don't we take a walk instead - see if we can find somewhere secluded?"   I hesitated.

There she was - all bouncing, coppery hair, smiling up at me with those bewitching, feline eyes. The pictures she conjured of lying together in long, dewy grass while light-filled leaves danced and swayed above us, enchanted my days and taunted my nights. In the breath of a summer breeze came whispers, and in the cool caress of her fingertips, warnings; yet still I'd wandered down the dark path of iniquity, led by the hand into the forest like a fairytale fool.   A life time ago.   Julia, of course, fussed when I arrived home early. "Flu? Well you do look pale. You've been over-doing it, if you ask me–"

I didn't ask you.

Her voice peck, peck, pecked at my head. "And you must remember you're getting on now. Why don't you think about retiring, Geoffrey?"

And on the phone to her sister, "Only I'm worried about him…not even reading the paper…not concentrating. Of course he won't go the doctor. He is one. Knows everything…"

There were days I'd wake up and look at this woman, and wonder how I had ever fallen in love with her. Eons ago our stars had been snuffed out and replaced with the endless, grey dawn of a dreary reality.

With Marlene, though, the light had been blinding. We found every spare moment, every inappropriate place, every excuse. To say I'd dreamt, yearned and longed for her would be an understatement. No description came close to the raw hormonal, unthinking force that propelled the stranger inside to act as he did.

Long after Julia had sunk into the soft oblivion of sleep, I'd lie starkly awake replaying every gasp, every touch, every throbbing pleasure in all its dizzying detail until I'd throw off the covers, waiting for the fever to abate. Which it had to, of course - love is just a chemical thing, after all, is it not? And it did – indeed it did…although not in a way I could ever have imagined.

It was the weekend of the August bank holiday when all three grown children came home with husbands, girlfriends, and toddlers. A heavy, airless day that sapped energy, blistered lawns and melted tarmac.

Marlene sent a text. She must see me and it was urgent.

Bloody selfish, I thought. She knew the family was here this weekend and now I had to sneak off like some kind of cad. Couldn't the woman spend just one day on her own?

She was waiting by the canal. Usual place. "Geoffrey. I'm so sorry but I had to–"

I looked at my watch. "Marlene, I've got the whole family here."

A tiny muscle twitched in her jaw. "What about me?"

"Oh come on - you know I'm married."

It caught me unaware. Suddenly her face crumpled. She dipped her head and began to rustle around in her bag. Out came a syringe. She caught my look and snapped, "Insulin."

"Oh! I didn't know."

"Hmm. Well my blood sugar's all over the place at the moment on account of my being pregnant."

Her mouth twisted into razor wire, the elfin face suddenly vixen. "I matter too you know, not just your wife."

'Wife' came out in a spit. And in an instant the fever I'd had all summer dropped, and my head cleared. Leaving a mind that began, with laser precision, to analyse the available options. All of them exacted a toll.

I took care, of course, to veil these thoughts, while offering the required words of comfort, put my arms around her and held her close. And later, in her flat, as she curled up beside me and slept with cat-like satisfaction - stretching, nestling and murmuring - I saw this needful child of hers - heard it fracturing the night with its screams…and snapped into decision.

A full vial of insulin sat on the bedside table. Laughably easy really – impossible to trace – and the perfect solution.

***

At least I thought it was. You see, I really hadn't banked on the woman haunting me. After her debut appearance that Saturday, Marlene's ghost followed me everywhere. During Monday's clinic I called for the next patient, looked up and there she was - seated on the consulting room couch.

A voice from far, far away, said, "Are you all right, Doctor?"

Still riveted to Marlene's image I barely heard the nurse.

"Do you want the next patient?"
Breathe, breathe...

Clinic seemed to run on interminably: the waddling, wheezing sick – old, smelly, stupid - or all of the above.

Afterwards, I grabbed my coat, dashed across the darkening, rainy car-park, sparked up the ignition and then stopped mid-flight. Turned. Oh, so slowly….Coming face to face with my passenger...Right next to me in the car…With bruises for eyes and dripping coils of blood-red hair. Such an enigmatic smile, as I screamed and clutched at my pounding chest. *Go away, go away, go away…*

Everywhere. She was everywhere. In the canteen queue. Lingering in an empty changing room. At the breakfast table next to Julia munching on cornflakes.   A month later I took annual leave. Guilt. What else could it be? I took sedatives. I pottered in the garden. Ate healthily. This would fade in time. Of course it would. Yet lying in bed I knew that if I opened my eyes she'd still be there - watching me while Julia turned the pages of her Margaret Atwood.

"Geoffrey, you're soaked," said Julia, peering over her bifocals.

I turned away. An old man. A frightened old man in sensible, striped pyjamas. "You look grey. Is it angina?"

What did she know? I was the God-damned doctor and it wasn't that.

Another week and I agreed to see Howard, a psychiatrist colleague. I was, by that time, pretty sure the visual hallucinations were symptoms of clinical depression. Howard nodded while I talked. Depression was, he agreed, a likely cause - the death of a lover, an encroaching retirement - it all made sense - and as he confirmed my diagnosis, relief washed over me. It could be treated. Thank God!

I returned home feeling more optimistic. After a hearty meal, I popped the first tablet and wandered into the bathroom, planning an early night. Only to find Marlene reclining in the bath. Corpse white. Lips the colour of crushed tomatoes, hair cascading like Ophelia. She smiled and held out her arms.

Another week and I was admitted to the psychiatric wing. The duty nurse took my blood pressure, clerking me in, when Marlene appeared at the end of the bed. I leapt back, gripping the sheets. Somebody was whimpering like a child. *Was that me? Was it? Was it me?*

The nurse stared.

"Do you see anything? Tell me you see something!"

Somewhere a door slammed, the echo drifting down the corridors along with the schooldays aroma of beef and boiled vegetables.

"Perhaps," she said, "a sedative, Geoffrey?"

"Sir." I reminded her.

More tests were taken. "We'll run the whole gamut," said Howard. "Give you a thorough MOT, old chap. Physical and psychological. I'm sure all you need is a bit of peace and quiet but we'll check you out properly nonetheless."

Behind Howard, Marlene sat playing with her hair, smiling to herself. *Breathe, breathe...*

"Do you believe in the hereafter?" I asked him, as she merged with the painting on the wall behind him, blending into its sea of bobbing boats.

Howard regarded me thoughtfully, his mind working through the list of possible diagnoses just like I would have done myself. "It takes time for the treatment to work, Geoff. Let's give it time."

I shook my head. Psychotic symptoms flirted erratically with pure madness, and my brain was all I had. A first-class, brilliant mind turning to jelly. A story of pity - students standing round my bed watching me dribble and giggle in a backless hospital gown – was that how I'd end up?

No, what this amounted to was guilt, pure and simple – festering and poisoning my mind, and it had to be lanced: a wound could never heal while still infected. Howard would understand that – the need to open up this hotbed of secrecy – and then once he knew the truth, he would be able to give me a soundly based second opinion. After all, he was duty-bound by patient confidentiality. Psychiatrists never divulged their patients' confessions, did they? I wasn't mad. Just eaten away with guilt. Of course...I could be well in no time...once cleansed... purged...

Behind Howard, Marlene nodded. It was the only way.

And the medical profession protected each other. Look how Marlene and I had covered each other's backs when the GMC asked questions.

And so, on the gathering rush of an impulse, I released my guilt. How in the early blue dawn I had taken a needle and slid it beneath Marlene's creamy skin. The woman was going to blast my world apart...

Howard nodded.

Two days later he came to give me the results of the tests he'd done. I stared with mounting horror while he calmly and almost apologetically explained that macular degeneration had caused something called De Bonnet's syndrome, which can result in highly disturbing hallucinations. The good news, however, was that it could be treated successfully.

I need not have confessed. Just one more day and I need not have confessed.

But worse - far, far worse - I should have known that, you see? I should have diagnosed myself for Christ's sake.

In the corner of my cell Marlene started to laugh quietly.

However, shortly after I began the course of treatment, she stopped laughing. Probably because I couldn't see her anymore. But then, I never saw my wife again either. Just four white walls and occasionally the prison warden's face peering through the grille in the door.

THE END

A Second Opinion was first published by: Ether books.com 2011

12. Retribution

The cell was sparse - just a table with two chairs positioned at opposite sides - and I was cold and fed up. "I've told you I can't explain. I don't know."

His hard, black stare bore right through me. "Try."

"You won't believe me. You'll think I'm making it all up so what's the use?" "Try me."

"It's Karen, not me - she's mad."

He raised a caterpillar eyebrow, his voice shot through with steel. "Start from the beginning, Lily. This is extremely serious. You do understand what a mess you're in, don't you?"

I nodded mutely as my stomach tumbled like a washing machine. When was it I had last eaten? Probably days ago. Certainly it felt like days. Or maybe hours. Without a window or clock I'd lost all track of time, but one thing I did know - there was no way I was getting out if I didn't talk.

I sighed heavily, shoulders slumped, picking at my nails. "Okay. Well we met on the training course about three months ago."

"Who?"

"Me and Karen. Well, Tamsin was on the course too, but it was Karen I hit it off with. Right away we were like, so close. She'd only have to look at me and I knew what she was thinking. Worrying really, now I know how mad she is. I mean - what does that say about me?" I laughed.

He didn't. "Go on."

"We really liked each other, that's all - found the same things funny. We had to sit through these God-awful training seminars from boring, pumped up pin-heads in suits. She'd say something like, 'I want to club him to death with my umbrella,' and I'd be doubled up because she had long, curly red hair and an umbrella with Pink Panther on it. So funny–" I looked into his impassive bulldog face and reckoned he'd had the old humour bypass. Still, in light of the situation... "No, okay, not nice. But funny. Yeah - funny. And like I said, I didn't know...I just got sort of sucked in. Look, it gets a bit tricky from here. Could I like, have a cup of tea or something?" "No."

"Right!" Jeez, my mouth was dry and what was coming up was going to make me sound like a freaking lunatic. "Right, well I'll just get it over with and you can think what you like, but I swear on my mother's life it's the truth, okay?"

"I hope you get on with your mother, Lily, because it had better be." "Yeah." I looked at him through strands of greasy hair. I felt awful, needed a shower. By then I just wanted to get out of there. "Okay, well this other girl, Tamsin Lewis, she really got on our nerves. I mean, she really, really grated. She was like, oh you know the type - short, tight skirts, always bending over and making doe eyes at the men. She did my head in. Right tart. If she had to stand up and do a presentation she'd be like sticking out her chest and tossing her hair about, eye-to-eye with Phil - he's our boss -

and ignoring everyone else. Of course we found out later the two of them were at it like-"

"At what?"

I squirmed. "*It*. We'd be staying away at a hotel, the whole team, and he'd be like, carrying her bags for her. I did, we did, you know - really hate her. And then once the course was over she got these amazing sales results when we knew she was a hopeless slag, and we had degrees and she didn't."

"And is that when you and Karen decided to teach her a lesson?"

"No. We didn't know how bad it was at that point, actually. It was about a month later when the bonus payments came out and she got £1500 while we got nothing. I mean - imagine - you're earning £12000 a year and you've got nothing left at the end of the month after tax and rent and bills... A quarterly bonus of £1500! Well that's a lot, mate." I could feel my face getting hot and that pressure cooker feeling inside again. Even after our revenge I was still incensed at the unfairness - the sheer injustice of what happened.

The man with the black eyes sat and waited. He was getting what he wanted. He knew it was coming - I could read him and I wanted to hold back but I couldn't: like a volcano lain dormant the eruption had started and it wasn't going to stop until it spewed. "Anyway, that's when she made her mistake. Tamsin. She told, and this is how stupid she is, she actually told Karen in a drunken bragging session in the bar that Phil had done her sales negotiations for her. Can you believe that? For a shag with that tart he sold *our* supplies into *her* wholesalers so *she* got the credit. So there Karen and I were - selling, selling, selling to all these shops and all the time they were buying from Tamsin's wholesalers because she had the better price. The whole thing stank." By then my fingers where clawing into my palms and my mouth felt so tight I was surprised the words could spit themselves out.

"So that was when–"

"When it started, yes."

And oh, boy did it start. As soon as Karen found out what was going on she motioned for me to drink up. We were going back to her place. She drove in total silence, chain smoking and gripping the wheel with little white claws. When we screeched into her driveway, she slammed the door shut so hard the car bounced. "Listen, Lily," she said, the second we were in through the front door. "We have to do something about that whinging little bitch."

A bottle of vodka later we were cackling away, pure venom pulsing through our arteries. No point going to Phil. He was the boss and to him sex spoke louder than anything we had to say on injustice.

"I'm going down the pan," Karen said, waving her cigarette around. "Flushed down the bog on a credit card."

"Me too."

"While Tamsin turns up dressed in cashmere and Karen Millen I can't even afford a splurge at Florence and Fred. No holiday this year, either."

I nodded, thinking of the week I'd hoped to have in the Grand Canaries and knew I'd be painting the spare bedroom instead. That £1500 would have paid off my card and bought me a week on a beach somewhere. "What shall we do? I mean it can't go on, can it?"

Karen broke into another bottle and passed me the fag packet. "Retribution."   "How?"

"Come with me."

I should have stopped then but every time I paused for breath I saw Tamsin's simpering smile. Heard her whiny voice telling Phil how she was 'going to go all the way' and when he smirked and glanced at the others in the team with a knowing look, she'd look all faux-innocent like she didn't know what she'd said.

"So there we were…"

The man with the black eyes stared at me unblinkingly. "Sitting in front of Karen's computer, right?"

I nodded.

"Be very careful now, Lily. You must tell me precisely what happened next. Leave nothing out."

"Okay. Well we were four sheets to the wind by then. And Karen had some pills she said were just herbal but I didn't care - I chucked one down my throat anyway with another shot of vodka on top. And then we were on this site. I remember we typed in, 'revenge.'"

I screwed up my face trying hard to recall the exact sequence of events. We'd both gasped when we saw what came up - a bright orange, fiery background and black capital letters with, 'Ultimate Retribution' emblazoned across it. We clicked to enter the site and selected, 'Injustice.' There were seven easy steps, it said, to initiate universal retribution. The cosmic laws of injustice must always balance, and it was our duty to right the wrong. Just seven easy steps and Tamsin would get her comeuppance. We loved it.

"Then once we were in we had to agree to the seven steps, which we did. Step One - that was easy - logging in and signing up. Karen logged in as Cruella and I was Boudicca. So funny. Then we typed in our details and moved onto Step Two. That was where we put in Tamsin's details - name, address, mobile, car registration, physical description. Actually it was quite comprehensive but we didn't care - we wanted someone to sort her out."

"Eliminate her?"

I squirmed again at that. "Well…..maybe just a good kicking."

"So you weren't clear?"

"Oh, we were at the time. We wanted her dead and buried, but of course we were drunk and high and–"

"And you're making excuses."

"Yes. No. Look, I'm just saying how it was, okay? After that we had to select the level of punishment required so we selected Death. Is that clear enough for you?" "You definitely selected Death?"

"Yes. Frankly we figured she deserved

everything she got. Anyway, after that it was onto Level Four. This was where we would be contacted by email and texts: when we received a question we must answer 'yes' or there would be negative consequences. We were asked if we understood and we clicked on 'yes.' Then we were asked to confirm, and we had to click 'yes' again. It was very exciting. Can't remember how I got home. Must have slept on Karen's floor."

The next day was a bit of a blur. It was a weekday and I was driving along a dual carriageway when my Carphone bleeped and I picked up a text. When I pulled over it was 'Darthveda' asking me if they should go ahead. Vaguely flashing back to the emphatic order to always say 'yes' when asked a question I texted back affirmative. This then happened several more times, and also by email when I logged on that evening. I remember texting Karen to ask her if she had also had these questions, and she texted back a smiley face with its tongue out, and I laughed.

I couldn't really remember much from the night before except we'd been on this weird website and it was all…well….adrenalin pumping, I suppose.

"Then some time during the night I got another text telling me I would start to see signs in the media - to look out for coded messages about Tamsin, that the Cosmos now knew she must be eliminated and it was up to me to do it. I have to say that scared me a bit. I was thinking that maybe Karen was a mad person. Like in a horror movie -

you know – and that it was her doing all this?"

"And did you receive these coded messages?"

"Yes."

"And then what? Level Five?"

"Uh-huh! I got an email the following day saying I had passed Level Four and now the Cosmos would exact retribution on Tamsin Lewis. I had to log on to the site again and sign in. I would then be able to choose the method of her destruction. At the time I was putting in my sales for the day and the whole thing was freaking me out, so I didn't do it. I thought the best thing would be for me to get another job or something. Walk away - you know–"

"Only you weren't allowed to?"

"No. I got a coded message to tell me I had signed a contract and must complete the course of action or the consequences to myself would come back a hundred fold."

The man nodded solemnly. "Go on."

"I remember waking at six the next morning with a heavy thump to the heart. I hadn't logged on and now something awful would happen to me. I managed to shrug off the feeling and shower, dress, have breakfast, but there was a sales meeting that morning and I was sinking with this overwhelming feeling of doom.

The first person I saw was a happy, smiling Tamsin showing off her engagement ring – to a junior doctor whose parents were buying them both a house as a wedding present. Karen and I raised our eyebrows at each other: obviously the poor sod didn't know she was screwing her married boss, then?

Phil then decided we should have a little quiz as a warm-up. The prize would be a Smart phone. And of course, Tamsin won it - just like she won the Amazon vouchers and the digital radio and everything else before it.

Anyway, straight afterwards, Karen and I met in the toilets.

"Tamsin knew the answers," Karen hissed as we washed our hands. "She and Phil met an hour early to 'go over her sales figures.'"

"Bloody bitch! Oh, that remind me - are you onto Level Six yet, Karen?" I asked, doing my lippy.

Our eyes met in the mirror and I knew that she was.

So that evening I logged on – with renewed determination, you might say! And for the method of destruction I chose 'Axe.'

"Level Six?"

I nodded. "Yes, and for this I had to send out texts to other retribution members, asking, 'Yes or No?' All the texts came back with a 'Yes' so I was through to the final stage. The instruction then was to log in immediately. It said I had ten 'Yes' votes, and to click on the final stage, which was, 'Confirm,' which I did. Good- bye, Tamsin! So, now can I have a cup of tea, please? I've told you everything."   "Not yet. So what happened next? To Tamsin?"

"Where's Karen, by the way? Have you got her here too?"

"Safe."

"Where?"

"She's told us everything, Lily so there's no point in lying."

"Karen's sick in the head. You have to believe me. She's been sending the texts all along, hasn't she? And the emails. She made me do it. She's as mad as a snake in a hot tin. I'm so glad I can see that now."

"Karen didn't send or receive any texts or emails, Lily. We've had her computer checked. She's clean."

There was a long pause while my world tipped on its axis. "What? So how did Tamsin? Oh, God - so who–?"

"That's what we'd like to find out, Lily. Your computer is clean too. And your phone. So all this business about a site called, 'Retribution' is - how can I put this politely? Um - bullshit. So I'll ask you one more time, Lily - who tried to kill Tamsin Lewis?"

Swirling senses falling through space and time… None of this was real anymore. It didn't make any sense what he was saying - no emails, no texts… Unless…and then it came to me - of course there weren't! All the evidence would have been wiped. That was part of the deal.

"Who almost murdered Tamsin, Lily? You or Karen?"

"Almost?"

"And we're very angry about that."

I stared back at him. He'd changed. No longer dark brown, his eyes were a brilliant emerald green, and much, much smaller. "We ve managed to wipe clean all yours and Karen's communication devices but the job still has to be completed. You and Karen slipped up somewhere and you're going to have to go through all seven stages again. Only this time more carefully."

"What? Who the hell are you?"

"Once you've tapped into the laws of universal retribution the deed must be carried out or the consequences will be dire for all of us - do you understand? You are messing with Lucifer himself!"

This whole thing was worse than I could ever have imagined. Everyone around me was a lunatic. I hardly heard the rest of what he said over the tirade of blood thumping through my head. "...and Tamsin must die soon before she regains consciousness and talks. The axe missed her jugular by–"

Wake up, Lily...wake up...

"You will now be taken for a rest and then we will start again and next time you must succeed–"

Vaguely I remembered being removed by a couple of heavies, before waking up here, in a room with faded orange curtains and someone sitting far too close on my bed, staring at me.

"You've been talking to yourself again," said the woman with wild, grey hair and a roll-up hanging off her lower lip. "All bloody night."

I sat up, looked around. The air smelled stale, like school dinners and pee. Oh, yes. I reached over and checked. Phew. The blue tablets they'd given me for my so-called psychosis were still safely stashed in my make-up bag. Good. Because I'll be out of here soon, and then I can go finish the job.

You can't mess around with the Universal Laws of Retribution, you see? You just can't. Tamsin Lewis *will* die. I promise you that.

THE END

***

Definition of schizophrenia: a mental disorder characterized by abnormalities in the perception or expression of reality. It most commonly manifests as auditory hallucinations, paranoid or bizarre delusions or disorganised speech and thinking in the context of significant social or occupational dysfunction. Onset of symptoms typically occurs in young adulthood with approx. 0.4-0.6 of the population affected.

Retribution was first published by: Ether books.com 2011

13. Moving In

The rat-a-tat-tat came late at night. Panicky. Urgent. Rosemary put down her paperback. The wind soughed in the trees outside and the fire crackled in the grate. Perhaps she'd imagined it. But then the knocking came again. Shaper and more insistent. *Let me in...Let me in...*

With a heavy sigh, she prised her creaking joints from the comfy armchair by the fire and shuffled painfully into the flag-stoned hallway with Paddy, the Labrador pattering behind, to unlatch the heavy oak door.

In a whirl of spiraling leaves and freezing fog, the visitor stepped into the old house, hair falling in a dark, silken sheath as the hood of her cloak dropped back. "I'm Alice," she said, holding out a slim, pale hand.

Rosemary's face creased into a frown of confusion.

"Your sister," explained the stranger. "You *are* Rosemary Fairfax?" "Sister?" She needed to sit down. She had no sister. This woman had made a mistake. But it was a dreadful night, so..."You'd better come through. Here - let me take your coat."

Then over cups of reviving tea, with firelight dancing on the walls, Alice began tell her story like a wicked stepmother reading an evil fairytale to a gullible child.

Rosemary's eyes widened and her heart fluttered wildly in her chest. This was just a bad dream, surely? If only she hadn't answered the door.

"Only you see, when my mother died there was nowhere for me to go. Just think - we must be about the same age, Rosemary!" Alice's dark eyes danced with amusement. Both women were sixty-two, yet while Rosemary was clearly a make-do-and-mend sort of woman cushioned with plenty of cream cakes, Alice looked like a fashion editor.

"I'm so sorry," said Rosemary, avoiding the unpalatable comparison. "Did your mother die recently?"

Alice nodded and the room appeared to darken. Abruptly she stood up and began to wander round the room, picking things up. This is nice and that is nice. As if calculating the value. "Nice place..."

"Well–"

"Our family house," she added, sitting down again with an impish grin.

Our? Rosemary's stomach plunged. Of course! If Alice was her father's illegitimate daughter from over sixty years ago then this woman would be here to claim her half of the house. But where did that leave herself? What ever would she do?

Pointedly, Alice looked at Rosemary's white knuckles gripping the chair. "Actually, Rosemary, you make me rather sick," she said, as calmly if she'd just said she loved the wallpaper.

"I beg your pardon?"

"Here you've lived your lovely life until the family house is handed over to you. You've never had to do a single day's work, have you, Rosemary?"

How far away from anywhere they were. With belts of thick sea mist rolling in over the fens, coiling wetly around the old house, stilling the trees and muffling sounds. A tight, small voice that Rosemary realised was her own, squeaked, "It's late. Perhaps you ought to go. We can discuss this another time."

"Oh, I don't think so." Alice poured herself another cup of tea. "At first he'd stay with us from Monday to Thursday, you know? No doubt your mother assumed he was at his club? Actually, sometimes he took my mother there." She smiled briefly. Before a thunderous cloud gathered behind her eyes and her voice hardened to flint. "But not often. No, you see usually, Rosemary, my mother would be sewing and sewing until her fingers bled. And in the evenings she'd sew some more for private clients - people like you - until her eyesight failed."

The smash of cup on saucer was sudden and violent, and a gasp echoed around the room. Rosemary's hands began to tremble and her teeth chattered like a child's. "I'm sorry." she said.

"You're sorry!"

"I didn't know."

"Neither did I. I didn't know about spoilt little Rosemary while my mother was taking in washing. Didn't know about the big house when we had a back yard terrace with damp crawling up the walls. He left us, Rosemary. Of course, I realise now that he was here all along with his comfortable country lifestyle and his fat little daughter–"

"Stop!" Tears sprung into Rosemary's eyes. *Fat little daughter…*"What do you want from me?"

Alice leaned back in her chair and gazed hypnotically into the flames. Then after what seemed an interminable age, she said, "What I want, Rosemary, is a home. A place to stay." Her words settled between them. "It's just that since Ma's gone there is nowhere, you see. For me."

"No."

"But now I've found you. My dear half-sister. And I'm sure it's what our father would have wanted, aren't you?"

Nausea clogged in Rosemary's throat.

Alice stood up. "Well now, I'll leave you to think on that, Rosemary."   Rosemary's body crumpled with relief. Alice was leaving. Going. With a bolted door behind her. Let the solicitor handle it now…

But after three fractured, sleepless nights she decided it would be best to take matters into her own hands. Alice must be plotting her next move and any day now a white envelope would arrive courtesy of an expensive London solicitor. She had to act fast - find out who Alice and her mother really were before outlaying money she could ill-afford. Such were her thoughts as the train trundled down to London.

The identity of Alice's mother, Ada, was easy to track down, on account of her having deceased recently; and further searching produced the births register for 1947. Ada had indeed had a little girl called Alice on the 17th November, and there, scrawled in thick, black italics for all the world to see, was evidence of her own father's betrayal. So Alice was who she said she was.

Goodness, she needed a stiff drink.

But there were no other children it seemed, and Ada had never married. How odd. Odder still that an attractive woman like Alice hadn't married either. Why? Why didn't she marry? Perhaps the answer could be found where they'd lived in East London? She glanced at her watch. There was time: she'd go there. With all those years at the same address, someone must know something?

Emerging from the tube station an hour later, Rosemary paused to question the wisdom of this decision, as dust bunnies of litter scurried across the deserted streets. Tap-tap-tap with her stick. All alone. Silly old fool. Should have left it to the solicitor. Who did she think she was - Miss Marple? Still, she was here now. Although, wholeheartedly she really wished that she wasn't.

Most of the pre-war terraces were now boarded up, and the one corner shop had grilles across the window. Ada's house, it transpired, was one of the few still lived in. But why would a smart, clearly successful woman like Alice want to live here? And for so long, too? Perhaps her mother had refused to move?

There was no answer when she knocked on

the door.

She looked around. Maybe a neighbour might remember Ada? Anything – just a clue to the truth, that was all… Eventually, a small, rotund Indian lady in a golden sari appeared at a window opposite. Their eyes met and Rosemary lifted up a hand to signal her distress. Her legs were heavy now and feeling the strain.

Fortunately the lady was kind and came to the door. "Oh yes, yes, you are friend of Ada… come in, come in. We'll take tea. It's just made in the pot."

"Oh, thank you. Thank you so much. It's been a longer trip than I thought. Silly to come all this way on my own, it really was. Oh, you're so kind…"

"No more tube for you," said the Indian lady, shaking a ring-laden finger as she showed Rosemary into a small, ornately furnished front room. "Not with those ankles. I will call you a taxi – my brother's firm – it's very good."

Gratefully Rosemary sipped the fragrant tea as she explained why she'd come. "Poor Miss Ada. I miss her very much. Such a lonely, unhappy old lady." "Lonely? But what about her daughter?"

Her host looked puzzled and shook her head repeatedly. "What daughter? She didn't have one."

"But she did. You see… Oh, it's a long story, and the taxi will be here in a minute, but well, the daughter came to visit me and it seems we're erm, half-sisters. I think, you know, after the war–"

The lady's brow creased. "No," she insisted. "No daughter. Miss Ada was very, very upset because the girl died of pneumonia at seventeen, you see? Alice, she called her. She never got over it and she never married. Poor Miss Ada. I used to do readings - kept her in touch with the other side. Oh, look my brother is here now with your taxi."

The train journey north passed in a blur of scenery as Rosemary struggled to comprehend what had happened. There would, after all, be no terrifying, crisp white letter falling on the mat; and no battle to keep the house.

Paddy looked up from his basket while Rosemary clattered around the kitchen preparing a late supper, muttering to herself. "I'm just a silly old sausage," she chuckled. "Must have dreamt the whole thing. Going senile, out here on my own,' she said to the dog.

And yet. The old house creaked so. A calm day and suddenly a door would slam, followed by the squeak, squeak, squeak of her father's old wheelchair working its way across an empty upstairs room. Tea-cups disappeared then re-appeared, and silvery voices whispered in corners.

Just the silly imaginings of an older woman, she repeatedly told herself. The strange mists rolling over the fens, an old house full of dark furniture, heavy paintings and family secrets….one which echoed to the tune of a turbulent past…that's all.

All the same, Rosemary decided to make

up a bed for Alice in the garden room. After that, sometimes, when she tottered up the path with a bag of shopping or a trug full of freshly dug vegetables, there would be a shadow at the window and the inescapable feeling of being watched. But there were no more late night visits and silence closed in once more.

Alice must, at last, be content Rosemary decided. Now that she'd moved in.

THE END

Moving In was first published by: Ether books.com 2012

14. Masquerade

The street party outside was setting her nerves on edge. Shouts too close to the windows - like a crazy, pitchfork wielding mob baying for blood.

Gwen, who was going through the cupboards in the bedroom upstairs, paused. Listened. Someone was climbing the steps up to the front door.

"Go away," she muttered under her breath. "Just go away."

The rat-a-tat-tat fractured the silence, echoing sharply round the house, gloomy now with the curtains drawn against the murky darkness. Shadows lurked on the walls like unearthly watchers. A floorboard creaked. Gwen held her breath. *Go away.* But the rat-a-tat-tat came again. Louder. More insistent. The fist of a man.

Gwen looked at the cat lazing on the bed and the cat looked back at her, ears flattened, not pleased at the disturbance to its tightly coiled sleep. The darkness, so thick it was almost a physical presence, pressed around her as she strained to hear. Good: the footsteps were retreating. Could she risk a peep between the curtains? Or would one of the revellers notice? Too risky.

She stayed stock-still, knees bent from sorting through boxes and clothing, as she mentally worked through the security situation: the curtains were closed downstairs, doors bolted from the inside, windows shut, a couple of lamps on. Surely the intruder would infer that no one was home? Everyone at the party? But those footsteps hadn't finished. Clomp, clomp, clomp. A squeal of the un-oiled side gate. Clomp, clomp, clomp. Round to the back door. Bolted, yes, but only glass. Thud, thud, thud! One gloved punch and he could be through...

Picturing a blurry face behind the frosted panes, and an ominous dark shape inches away on the other side, Gwen's hands squeezed into white-knuckled claws, her heart pulsing hard in her throat, her neck. *Oh please, please - just go away*.

What made this person think everyone wanted to party, anyway? To sing and dance with painted faces and ghoulish costumes? Couldn't they leave people alone and let them make their own decisions?

The event had certainly been publicised well enough - no one could possibly have missed all the posters and leaflets. There had been cards in the shop windows, banners strung from lampposts, and schoolchildren banging on doors selling tickets - it was tricky avoiding the little blighters! No, everyone would know about tonight's party in the park with its fireworks and loud music. And most were going.

"There were never things like this when I was a girl," she said softly to the cat, who stared at her as if she was out of her tree. "I blame America."

The cat yawned and stretched, kicked and

wriggled a little, then curled up to resume where he left off - satisfied that the crisis was over.

Deeming it safe but just to make sure, she stood on creaky knees and edged towards the window to peer hesitantly round the edge of the curtain. With a start she jumped back - a warrior with a spear was plodding back up the driveway, leaving the side gate swinging open. Charming! Still - at least he'd gone. Good.

A low mist had settled in, swirling around lanterns and torches like spectres in the night. Against the yellow fuzz of the streetlights, a fine spray of determined drizzle was dampening glittery costumes and banners, but not spirits. The mass of bodies swayed as one, moving like a giant centipede down the street towards the park opposite - lanterns dancing, pointy hats bobbing, children in fancy dress laughing and shouting, "Everybody out! Party, party, party!"

Gwen let the curtain swing back into place. They ought to know - not everyone wanted to party, thank you very much.

It hadn't always been this way. Once her home had been a beacon of family warmth - the thunder of tiny feet on the stairs, doors slamming with petulant, 'It's not fair, but why can't I?' tantrums. Doors flung open on balmy summer evenings and always something freshly cooked waiting from the kitchen for the boys after football practice. Sometimes, on winter evenings, George would light a real fire and they'd make toast over it with George's mother's old toasting fork.

"We had to do this when I was a kid," he'd

tell his wide-eyed sons.

"What - you mean you didn't have a toaster?"

"Nope. Nor a dishwasher, nor a microwave or even a colour television."

They started to laugh. "Dad, you're making all this up!"

"He's just teasing, Tom - don't believe him."

"And we certainly didn't have central heating," George went on, warming to his theme, "My mother used to put hot bricks in the bed in winter."

Gwen smiled sadly as she made a start on the dressing table drawers. They hadn't had much money, not on George's wages as a cab driver and she a full time mother, but they had laughed a lot - a close and happy family. And enjoyed simple pleasures like playing a game of Monopoly or sharing a homemade chocolate cake while they watched Saturday night television - good in those days, she remembered, lots to make you laugh. Not like today's obsession with crime and hospital traumas.   She worked swiftly. Clearing. Sorting the wheat from the chaff. The time had come, and it all boiled down to this - what could be sold? And God alone knew, she needed the money.

A tidal wave of rage threatened to engulf her yet again, making her head spin and her fingers fly faster. She shouldn't have to do this, especially not at her age. This should have been a golden time of reward, of holidays and grandchildren, a time she had looked forward to after years of washing underwear and sports kits, of scrubbing the grimy bathroom and picking up wet towels. Now this. Damn George, upping and leaving after all those years, taking his redundancy money and his fancy piece 'for a new life in America.' *Thanks George. Thanks a sodding bunch!*

Maybe she'd brought up the boys a little too well? Alfie had graduated from university with a first class degree, which had opened up a top job for him in London. And Tom had disappeared - backpacking in the Far East, where he was now teaching English and planning to marry a local girl. All of which left her here alone - rattling around in a house whose ceilings seemed to reach ever higher and whose rooms were expanding. A house she could no longer afford, kitchen drawers crammed with letters written in red ink, wallpaper peeling and rugs frayed. The boys would be appalled if they knew to what level their mother had sunk.

Nearly finished. Gwen sat back and gazed at herself in the dressing table mirror, ghostly in the lamplight: pockets of sadness under her eyes, pinched mouth - sucking lemons as George used to say - and a turkey wattle neck. She pinched the tissue skin over her voice box. It stayed in the pinched position - a tiny peak of crepe. So here she was - resorting to selling possessions in markets and on the internet, counting out small change so she had enough to eat. And now the house was going - repossession. *Thanks, George.*

Still, the dirty job was almost done. Gwen

stood up. The first firecracker made her jump as if a gun had gone off and she had to steady herself. Crack. Crack. Crack! The cat flew off the bed in a streak of fur. A cacophony of fireworks fizzed and a cheer went up. Then came the bumf, bumf, bumf of pounding music. Through the curtains she could see the bursts of colour exploding in the sky, and almost smell the smoke, sizzling hot-dogs and frying onions. Tears stung her eyes. Party time. Parents holding onto tiny, excited hands. Faces aglow as the fireworks flew, popped and sparkled, lighting up the black night in a brilliant blaze.

Get a grip, Gwen. Finish the job.

Quickly she placed everything saleable into a large rucksack and then padded quietly downstairs. In the kitchen she shrugged into her black hoodie and picked up her ghoulish party mask and torch. Then slid out of the back door and melted into the throng unnoticed.

A street party. Everybody out. A good night for cat burglars, then? And tonight there would be rich pickings.

THE END

A version of Masquerade was first published by My Weekly November 2011

15. Adele

There she lies, skin white as alabaster, as perfect in death as she was in life.

"I'll leave you then - for a few minutes," the mortuary assistant says in hushed tones, barely above a whisper.

The door shuts softly behind me. We are alone, Adele and I, with the humming emptiness of the morgue. Perhaps her spirit watches me from somewhere above my head, peeping over the water pipes, as I shuffle towards her still, statue like body. I wonder what she sees. All that warm pulsing passion, now swept cruelly away to leave a tear stained straggly haired youth in an ill-fitting suit, flailing around hopelessly without her. My beautiful Adele.

I bend to kiss her cool marble forehead. Unreal. See the curve of her immaculate eyebrows - like inverted ticks - the elegance of her long, feline eyes, and the soft fan of black lashes on sculpted cheeks. The fullness of her plump cushioned lips draws me towards them but no, wait. They will be cold. She is dead. Adele is dead. No more the crush of heated, pulsating skin. No more the heaving of her body against mine. Adele is dead, dead, dead.

I drop my gaze, feeling a cool draft of air against my clammy skin, clearing my head, lifting the nausea. It wafts over the white sheet that covers her body from the neck down, rippling over the swell of her breasts down to the hollow of her stomach, clinging to bony hips and long, slender thighs. Would her toenails still be painted in the blackberry polish I varnished them with less than two nights before? Sometimes they'd be blazing red, other times gothic black or candy pink.

"Paint them," she'd say, flinging herself onto the sofa next to me in the middle of a football match, long, bronzed legs draped across my lap. "Come on, Guy, you do it so well," with a cat-like knowing smile. Of course, I couldn't resist. I never could, not from the first moment I set eyes on her.

Adele had been a model, whereas I, well, I suppose you could say I was ordinary - training to be a solicitor, mid-twenties, played football or rugby at weekends, drank in the local pub with a crowd I'd known since school. I was one of those people who never expected much to happen. I'd been seeing Dawn, who works in the bakery, for a few months but all that changed the night Adele walked into the pub. Pow! Imagine a comic character with his eyes popping out on alarm clock springs from his eyeballs. Imagine heart signs in neon pink pinging from his chest. Imagine all conversation ceasing. That was the Adele effect.

No one could quite work out why she picked me, though. She said she was a receptionist. At twenty-eight too old to be a photographic model anymore.

"Rubbish," I told her, running my hot, eager hands down her naked back. "You still put the rest of them in the shade."

She'd smiled and purred, incredibly, unbelievably, happy in my bed with me, in my two-bedroom terrace house.

There was just the one thing that bothered me, though - the gloves.

"I can still do hands," she said, explaining their presence shortly after we first met. "That's why I wear these. Don't ever make me take them off, okay? They've got to be milky white perfect or I don't get work."

She always wore them - white cotton usually – and black satin in the evenings. They added a slightly old fashioned, lady-like touch to her glamorous image, like a latter day Audrey Hepburn or Princess Grace. And at first I didn't mind. It was one of her eccentricities.

I knew, of course, that she'd had her breasts enlarged. She openly admitted it. The lads down the pub called her Jordan. And of course she'd had her teeth done, no denying that when they flashed dazzling, blue-white in between her pouty lips. It didn't matter. Adele was stunning. If she'd had a bit of enhancement, so what? She was a model; it was her line of work. And she was a beautiful woman - all mine. Or was. The real mystery, as people kept reminding me, was why on earth a woman like that had ever wanted to marry me.

'He must have money.' I heard the whispers. It insulted me. But worse, it insulted her. What we had, whether the gossips liked it or not, was love. It was me who wanted to marry her not the other way round. And me who tried to persuade her to model again.

"No – no more publicity, Guy," she'd say, cuddling up beside me on the sofa. "Just you and me, that's all I want."

She was content with me, you see, enjoyed me fussing around after her, running her baths, painting her nails...

I can still see her the day she moved in, surrounded by designer luggage, cat eyes flashing, long, blonde hair cascading down her back to skin pinching white jeans. Cote d'azure meets Rotherham. It was raining outside, spattering the window, dirty brown streets with people running to their cars. The image was surreal, haunting, and will stay with me forever.

In contrast to her everything in my house suddenly looked old and shabby. Adele wanted new. We'd have it, I told her. One day I'll be a corporate lawyer and you'll have everything. Oh, how her eyes shined at that. All new.

"I'll buy you a mansion," I said, "a gothic palace." She loved it. Anything oddball, unusual, eccentric. It was one of the many things I adored about her - that what you think she was she wasn't, that what you saw you didn't necessarily get. I loved everything about her. Except those gloves. I began to not like those.

I wanted, begged, to feel the caress of her fingers on my skin, to see the glint of my ring on her finger.

She'd smiled enigmatically, touched my face with a cotton-cool hand. "I don't need a ring," she said. "Just you."

That last night we'd danced, bodies brushing, lights down low. And the next day she would have been my wife. Except she collapsed in my arms.

"Ah!" The door behind me swings open and I spin round to face a balding man holding a pile of notes in a file. He eyes me for too long a moment over heavily rimmed glasses, a slight knotting of the brows, while his voice echoes around the room, bouncing off tiles, piercing the gloom of my thoughts. "You must be the son?"

I look at him askance.

"I take it you are the next of kin?" he asks.

"Son?" What son? There were no children. Besides, at six foot two I could hardly be mistaken for any pre-pubescent schoolboy. Of course, he has the wrong room, wrong patient, wrong body…. Oh, God preserve us from bureaucratic incompetence. My voice is snappy, harsh. "No - no children. I'm Adele's fiancé."

Now his brows leap together to form a long black line. He checks his details again. "Adele Watson, right?"

"Correct."

"Born fifth September 1950?"

"No!" For Christ's sake! "She's only twenty-nine."

Confusion swirls, catching us in its chilly breeze. We stare at each other. I can feel my nostrils flaring. How can this idiot be so badly informed, so insensitive?   And then something in his expression changes and softens. "Ah, I see."

He gestures to a chair.

I ignore him.

There is a touch at my elbow. I shrug him off.

"She went suddenly, didn't she? I'm afraid her poor body couldn't take anymore."

"Couldn't take what anymore?" My mind's working fast now - thinking drugs or secret drinking…Oh Lord, what hasn't she told me? "They said she had a weak heart?"

"Well her heart couldn't take any more, that's for sure. Not after the last lot of liposuction. I take it you knew about that?"

I shake my head. I am vacant, empty headed - nothing makes sense.

He moves swiftly on. "There was an infection. It seemed the antibiotics didn't work. They tried almost everything on the spectrum but nothing– She was taking painkillers like smarties."

"Liposuction? Painkillers?" Perhaps it was the honeymoon in the Caribbean that made her do it? Adele, ever the perfectionist, must have wanted to look even better than she already did. Why, oh why? She was perfect to me. My thoughts are racing, so much so I barely hear what he says next.

"You didn't know? Ah," he says again, clearing his throat rather awkwardly. "Well, ah-hem, she'd had rather a lot of surgery in the last few years–' And he begins a litany as if reciting from a catalogue. "…a face-lift, a brow lift, a neck lift, dermabrasion, laser resurfacing, a breast augmentation. Twice. Underarms tucked, liposuction to the abdomen and thighs, cosmetic dentistry with full implants upper and lower. Ah yes, and Botox. It's all here. I'm afraid she must have been rather, er, frugal with the truth. She was fifty-seven."

Swaying sickeningly, I clutch at the table she lies on.

"Look," he says, lifting the sheet to take one of her delicate hands in his. It is crinkled like used tissue paper, creepy and blotched with light brown shapes. It is the hand of an old lady. The one part of herself she could do nothing about. "Did you never look at her hands?"

It is only then that I let myself see the tiny, white scars tucked beneath the hairline of rich, golden hair, the telltale fine silvery threads that run deep beneath the golden tan, tracing along the inside of her arms and her tanned, toned belly. Only then that I see how fragile the image. And only then I realise what she had seen in me - and wanted so badly. My youth.

The End

Adele was first published by: 1. Scribble, Park Publications 2008, 2. Mosaic - anthology by Bridge House Publishing 2010 3. Ether books.com 2012.

16. Night Duty

Strange things happen in hospitals during the early hours. I should know - I've been working nights for long enough.

There's something timeless about the long, grey hours of dawn that makes people feel disorientated: who are they? Where are they? Often I'd be on my rounds and find a befuddled patient in the sluice looking for a kettle! Or determined to get dressed because they're late for work. It would take a minute before they remembered - oh yes, still in hospital, got a drip up. Back to bed. Back to sleep. Just a bad dream.

Tonight Tessa's in charge. She sits knitting - click-clack-click-clack- whilst chatting to the tea-lady, Beryl, who's just finished washing up the cocoa mugs. Leaving me, as usual, to walk round the ward checking up on the patients. Tessa, to be blunt, is lazy - she works a couple of nights a week for the better rate of pay, then does as little as possible while she's here. She's not dedicated like me. For me this is a vocation: a calling. The way it should be.

First there's old Mr Betts - in my opinion they should never have operated at his age. At home he could manage but now he's got a nasty chest infection and doesn't know where he is. They asked him, shouting into his one good ear, "Do you know where you are, Arthur?"

"Aye," he shouted back. "I'm in bed."

Not lost his fighting spirit then! On a waiting list, he's now down for residential care. Gaunt and wheezy, he lies staring at the ceiling, listening to the hiss of oxygen and asking for his late wife. "Where's my Lily? Are you Lily?"

I squeeze his hand. "Lily's here." It's best.

And then there is Isobel. Isobel was a lively schoolteacher. Now look - with creeping inevitability, Isobel is fading to grey, her cold, tissue fingers reaching for mine. I'm glad I'm here, whispering, reassuring, to take her through the darkest hours. I end with Joe in the side ward - there because he relives the battlefields, groaning and shouting. It keeps the others awake. "Joe. I'm here now. It's all right." His young, hazel eyes widen, confused and then relieved. It's just night time. "Don't leave me, Nancy. Stay with me."

I pull up a chair and hold his hand. "Of course."

"Promise?"

Tucking in his blankets, I whisper, "Promise."

When I finally drift back to the nurse's station, Tessa is telling the night sister ghost stories. The poor night sister will later have to walk alone down the draughty corridors of the old District General as she visits the other wards, her footsteps echoing eerily on the cracked tiles. At each sigh of wind or rattling window pane, she will shoot nervous little glances over her shoulder - walking quickly past the operating suites, now acutely aware of the patient who once escaped from the morgue, and the vengeful hospital porter who stalks the deserted basement. She shudders as Tessa laughs gleefully - clickety-clack-clickety-clack.

"How's Arthur Betts?" Sister asks, checking her notebook.

Tessa carries on knitting. "Oxygen on. Propped up. Obs okay."

Sister nods. "Isobel?"

"Yeah, fine."

"And how's the heating in those side wards? Is it fixed yet? Have we got enough blankets?"

Behind Sister I shake my head but Tessa ignores me. "Still freezing. We've got blankets, though. We've done our best."

I glare at Tessa as she peers over Sister's shoulder and frowns at me.

"Well, best get on," says Sister. "Wish you hadn't spooked me, though. I'll be terrified all night now."

Tessa laughs and carries on knitting. Eventually she looks at her watch and stretches. "Ooh - time for a break," she says, wandering into the kitchen to make herself a coffee.

A break!

In the day room sit the insomniacs, watching shadows flicker along the walls. Outside, fog swirls around buttery lamplights and dark streets glisten damply. Huddled in dressing gowns the talk is of loosely grasped politics and lives of rough work, jobs which have left them with hardened lungs, greying skin and hollow eyes. I pull my cloak around me and settle into one of the armchairs at the back of the room for forty winks. Five o'clock is always the most difficult time to stay awake. The two old men, muttering about the cold, shuffle back to their plastic mattresses and thin sheets. Strange, this hour between night and dawn: with the body slow and the mind playing tricks. I drift in and out of a dream-filled slumber, suddenly jumping alert with a feeling of déjà-vu.

Still dark out there, but silvery fingers are creeping through the blinds and there comes the distant clatter of the medicine trolley. It must be six o'clock already. Goodness - Tessa is doing some work! Tea-cups rattle and beds creak as sleep-fuddled patients struggle to prop themselves up or plod towards the bathroom. Lights flick on. Blinds roll up. A new day. Sometimes I feel so darned weary I could just roll over and forget the world, but there is work to be done. And my first thought is Joe.   He's fast asleep. For once no murmurings or kicking. I tuck the blankets back up to his chin and sit watching him for a while. Okay, you've gathered - I've got a soft spot for him. But Joe is the reason I became a nurse - to look after people who are damaged and traumatised. And who else is going to care for him like I do? Who else will sit through the night and hold his hand when he cries out? Most nurses would rather be at home with their families or tucked up in bed asleep. There aren't many like me these days.

Tessa, having dispensed the medicines and filled in a few charts with fictional temperatures and blood pressures, pens the notes (slept well, slept well, slept well ...) before disappearing for a quick breakfast prior to the day staff arriving.

Me? I move on to Isobel and old Mr Betts. They are tired now. The night has been a long one for them especially. Tea cups sit untouched and I pull up blankets, smooth brows and let them sleep on. My work, for the night, is done.

At the end of the shift, I'm just in Sister's office when the door opens.

"She was here again last night," says the night sister to the day sister. "I'm sure of it."

"Who? The Angel?"

Night Sister nods. "The two old chaps in the dayroom said the air was freezing in there."

"Well, the heating's on the blink again, Sister."

"I know - but both Mr Betts and Isobel dying in one night? And some of the patients said they saw a figure drifting around the beds in a long dress. And that side ward is perishing. No wonder no one will sleep in there. Poor Beryl dropped the tea-tray again this morning - said she saw a grey figure slip out through the door!"

"I think Tessa's been up to her old tricks again with those ghost stories - you look as white as a sheet. Both of those patients were extremely ill! Have the relatives been told? Good. Anyway, you know how it is in the early hours with strange noises and apparitions! Strong painkillers or a few stories and everyone thinks they can see ghosts on the ward."

Well she's right there, I think. They certainly

do. And I should know. I've been here for over eighty-odd years now. And I've seen enough startled faces and mouths dropping open to know for sure that they do.

Anyway, I'll leave them now to discuss their ghosts. For me it's back to the side ward to sit with Joe. He needs me and I'll always be here for him. Waiting, and willing him to recover. I promised, you see, when he begged me all those years ago - in his darkest hour.

"Don't leave me will you, Nancy? Promise you'll be there when I wake up?"

"Of course I will." He was the reason I came here, like I said. We were going to marry before the second world war broke out, you see.

And I never break my promises. I'll never leave my Joe.

THE END

Night Duty was first published by Woman's Weekly, October 2011

17. Rosie and Joe

Rosie stared through the stained glass of the magnificent oriel window in the Great Hall, and sighed at the darkening sky and flurry of dead leaves being chased across   the lawns. A storm was blowing in, of that she was certain, and still no sign of any visitors.

She glanced over at the Grandfather clock tick-tocking methodically against the linen-fold panelling on the far wall - four o'clock - and walked over to prod at the log fire, which crackled and hissed in the grate. In the room across from the Hall, clattering crockery and raised voices signalled that preparations for tonight's dinner were already well underway. Part of Rosie's job was to show visitors to Melhampton House their rooms upstairs. But time was pushing on and she'd been at work since early that morning. Rain had started to pelt the windows, splattering sideways in harsh bursts, leaving trails of rivulets to run down the panes. She threw another log onto the fire, thinking about the small room and single bed she would soon return to, and how lonely she sometimes felt in the long, dark winter nights, when a deep, male voice behind her left shoulder made her jump.

Rosie whirled round. "Ooh, Sir, you gave me such a fright."

The man laughed, throwing back a head of

rich, black curls. She eyed him more closely, realising he was younger than she'd first thought - twenty, perhaps - much the same age as herself; and a hot blush slowly suffused her skin.

"Joe," he said, holding out his hand. "Joe Rothwell." He gestured to one of the silk upholstered sofas either side of the fire, and they sat down, staring at the Flemish tapestry between them in tongue-tied silence.

Joe's physical presence seemed to fill the room, and Rosie's eyes were being drawn to his. Immediately she looked away again, much to his obvious amusement. Oh dear, she should ask him something, like, 'where are the others?' or maybe introduce herself like she normally would, but every time she tried her throat constricted. The silence between them stretched and stretched, his warm, honey brown eyes searching her profile, willing her to look at him.

"You have a nasty cough," he said.

"Have I?" She hadn't realised she'd been coughing, since it was as regular as breathing these days.

The light outside was now fading fast, rain setting in, heavy and solid, dripping profusely from overflowing guttering and pipes. She ought to light the candelabra on the oak table. If only he wasn't staring quite so much. Eventually she forced herself to raise her eyes to his.

Joe smiled broadly. "So, er…."
"Rosie."
"How enchanting. Rosie."
Rosie blushed some more.

"Your name suits you. Ah-hum… So, they say this place is haunted. Is it true?" "Oh yes," said Rosie, slightly more comfortable now they were on her favourite subject - the history of the house. "There's the Grey Lady. She's said to wander round the rose garden. And two gentlemen fighting a duel on the galleried landing. I've never seen them, though, and I've been here for years."

"Really? And I've never seen you."

"I've never seen you, either." It felt as though she'd drunk a couple of glasses of strong wine too quickly, or woken abruptly from a dream - that feeling of static stillness, being aware of every thumping heartbeat, every firing nerve… Who was this man who thought she should know him?

"I come here to visit Wills."

She barely registered what he was saying.

"He lets me use the Gatehouse to write in. I'm a poet. Perhaps I shouldn't say that, with only one collection published, or shortly to be…."

Joe… A poet….visiting…

A violent gust of wind suddenly whistled through the trees, thrashing the walls of the house and sweeping down the chimney so that smoke billowed into the room. Rosie began to cough again, and Joe jumped to her side and reached for her hand.

"Wild night."

He was oh so close, his hand folding her tiny cold one in his like a velvet glove. The desire to lean into him as if they had known each other all their lives was overwhelming. And really very, very silly.

Rosie stood up. "Can I get you some tea, Joe?"

He blinked, long dark lashes feathering momentarily against ivory skin, the corners of his elegant lips twitching mischievously. "Tea? Well then, how about some hot wine instead?"

Rosie pursed her lips. "I'll bring tea."

Whatever would the mistress say if she found her with a young man, drinking wine? Yet the smile she knew was spreading across her face remained, as she bustled through the 15th century archway to the ante-room, and from there down a spiral stone stairway to the kitchens.

Downstairs the intoxicating aroma of roasting venison and baked sponge filled her nostrils while she hunted for the tea set - people were always moving things to where she couldn't find them – and turned over in her mind the conversation with Joe.   Unnoticed amid the pandemonium in the kitchen, she made the tea, setting the tray with cream and sugar and a plate of scones and teacakes, then with trembling hands and racing heart, hurried back up to the Great Hall.

Except for the fire, it was now quite dark. She set down the tray on the oak table in the centre of the room and lit the candelabra.

"There, that's better…"

But Joe had gone.

She stared at the sofa where he'd been sitting only moments ago. Perhaps he'd sneaked off to the wine cellar next to the kitchen? Picking up the candelabra, she made towards it. The cellar, fully stocked and stacked with cases waiting to be unloaded, however, remained eerily quiet. Marching back into the Great Hall, she hurried up the spiral Jacobean staircase by the oriel window. The library too, was empty. As was the King's Room, and the State Bedroom. She threw open every door down the corridor, flying from one room to the next - the Dressing Room, the secret passageway to the Chapel, the Yellow Room...knowing, yet needing to check anyway, that he wasn't going to be in any of them, that he had disappeared. Joe, quite simply, had disappeared.

And it was at that point, as Rosie resignedly plodded back down to the Great Hall, that something he'd said began to replay in her mind: *Wills lets me use the Gatehouse.* She didn't know a 'Wills.' And secondly, and far more disturbingly - the Gatehouse had been demolished in 1862, nearly forty years before.

***

Joe hurriedly let himself into the Gatehouse, bedraggled and soaked to the bones after his sprint outside. Rubbing his hands together he darted towards the small writing desk by the window, and quickly lit a candle so he could see to light the fire and search for that small bottle of brandy he knew he had somewhere. Finally slumping into the armchair by the fire he took a swig of liquor and forced himself to take calming, deep breaths. She was beautiful, the most exquisite creature he'd ever laid eyes on - flaxen hair, skin so translucent he couldn't stop staring at her - and yet….he'd known there was something odd about her, something ethereal, cold, and unreachable. He took another long swig. Darn it, had she really walked straight through the wall? When his heart finally stopped banging against the wall of his chest, he shook his head. No, he'd been dreaming, tired after the long journey… What he had do was go back – he really must - and find out. He certainly couldn't let this rest.

***

Angela Phillips looked around at her assembled dinner guests in the Great Hall, and smiled. Everything was perfect - right down to the roaring fire and stormy night buffeting the 18 inch stone walls and rattling window panes. While the guests sipped mulled wine, she let her eyes roam around the 15th century Hall, noting the floor to ceiling family portraits of Nicholas's ancestors, who could be traced back for over five hundred years, the Flemish tapestry over the fireplace and oh… a cold draught caused her to shudder. Strange, the heating was on full and the fire blazing.

"I hear you have ghosts here?" A man was asking.

Laughter tinkled around the room as all eyes turned towards her.

Angela smiled in response. "Of course, we

do. In fact we have so many I'm surprised they don't bump into each other. There's the Grey Lady who wanders round the rose garden; a couple of gentlemen fighting on the landing; and a naughty housemaid who you can sometimes hear coughing - she leaves all the doors open upstairs as if she's looking for someone. And then there's a young man with heavy boots and wild black curls who stomps up and down the Great Hall here. Only on dark, rainy winter afternoons, though."

"Like today?"

"Yes," said Angela brightly. "Exactly like today."

THE END

Rosie and Joe was first published by: 1. My Weekly 15/11/2008 and 2. Ether books.com 2012

18. Sixty Seconds

60 seconds and the whole thing will be over. Helen bites her lip and grips the steering wheel. Kirsty steps off the pavement, blonde hair curling in the early evening drizzle. She turns to face the oncoming car.

Do it. Time's running out. Just do it…Do it - Now!

***

They'd been at school together and only re-met when Kirsty brought her elderly aunt in to the nursing home that Helen managed.

"Come and have a drink after work," said Kirsty, wandering round Helen's office, picking up ornaments then putting them down again - not quite in the same place they'd been before. Her gaze eventually settled on a photograph of Helen's son. "Now there's a handsome boy."

Helen smiled proudly. "My son, Jamie. He's off to university next month."

"Yours and Rob's boy? Well, well - Rob always did have good looks. You dropped lucky there, Helen."

Helen's smile faded a little.

"Anyway, must dash. Things to do and all that. Come if you can - it would be lovely to have a catch up!"

Kirsty's stilettos click-clacked sharply across

the foyer. An engine roared to life outside the window. Gravel flew. And the day darkened.

The afternoon was a busy one with several new admissions followed by a fire in the kitchen. And at six o'clock, Helen's reflection in the office mirror told her that an early night would be a far more sensible option than going to a city bar to meet an old school friend she hadn't seen in over thirty years. Especially such a glamorous one - wouldn't she feel a frump?

Rain spattered against the windows, and the aroma of boiled vegetables and gravy wafted down the corridors in a pungent reminder of school days. She and Kirsty had never even been close. Kirsty was the girl who whispered behind your back making another girl giggle. Then she'd grin and say, "What? I didn't say anything!" Kirsty had been the first girl in class to get white, knee boots. The first to own a record player. And the first to be kissed by Darren Mathews, a tough boy with dark hair and a dimpled grin. All the girls wanted to be kissed by Darren but Kirsty was the one he chose. Or did he? With the benefit of hindsight, Helen wondered about that. Still - it would be nice to find out what had happened to some of her old classmates, and she could hardly leave the poor woman waiting alone in a city centre bar, could she? Helen fluffed up her short, greying hair as best she could and applied a smudge of lipstick. She'd go.   But it wasn't until the occasional catch-up had turned into regular drop-ins that she became suspicious. They had little in common - Kirsty was a childless divorcee with a high-powered career - and few shared interests, Kirsty being into fashion and parties, and Helen preferring to garden or read.

Then one day when Helen was bending over the weekly staff rota deep in thought, Kirsty bounced into her office for the fourth time that month. Helen took off her glasses and suppressed a deep sigh.

"Just popped in to see Auntie," said Kirsty. "Thought I'd say hi. So, how are you, Helen?" She flung herself onto the chair opposite and plonked her designer handbag on the floor. "You look dreadfully tired, dear. You ought to treat yourself to a facial. I swear by them."

"Kirsty!" said Helen through gritted teeth. "How nice to see you."

"Could we get some coffee, do you think? Will someone bring us some?"

"I'll get it. Sugar?"

"God, no!"

"So how are things, Kirsty?" Helen looked at her watch. She really was extremely busy. "I've got a few minutes for a break but not long if you don't mind."   "Not at all." Kirsty took off her long, cream coat and tossed it onto the sofa behind her. "Truth be told I just need someone to talk to. Other women are always so busy with their boring family squabbles." Here she raised her eyes to the ceiling. "Oh, and I've split up with Carl. Do you remember me telling you about him?"

Helen took a sip of coffee and tried to recall who Kirsty's latest boyfriend was. Something about him being a student or having a lot in common with her son, Jamie, and wouldn't it be great if they could meet up? Something like that. She did know she'd managed to avoid the foursome where her son would be the same age as Kirsty's partner. At least now that particular nightmare - where she and Rob would feel like elderly relations - was over.

She tuned back in while trying to keep an eye on the clock. All the medicines still had to be dispensed to the residents and she had an appointment with a catering manager in less than an hour.

"....so I was wondering if I could stay over at yours for a while. At least until he's gone. I've told the boy to be packed and out within the week. All the tears and tantrums, honestly, when a relationship's run its course, its run its course–"

Helen frowned. This boy was only a couple of years older than Jamie. Perhaps Kirsty had forgotten how raw feelings could be at that age. Jamie had split with his girlfriend last summer. She recalled his wracking sobs through the bedroom walls. When she went into his room he'd reached out to her like a broken child and she'd rocked him to sleep. After that he refused to go to university, get a job or even go out with his friend, Steve. It had taken months for him to agree that his life mattered and the decisions he made now would have a lasting impact.

They were now on solid ground again but his emotions still swung alarmingly. Poor Carl. She hoped he had somewhere to go.

"…and what I can't stand about him is the

way he just stares at me. I said, 'It's like, so over. Get a life. Time to move on.' What a body though! Helen - don't look so shocked." Kirsty glanced at her watch. "Oops, look at the time." She reached for her coat. "So if I come over on Friday? About six? I'll take you and Rob out for dinner, of course."

Annoyance clouded Helen's features as more smiles and air kisses were bestowed on her. At what point had she agreed to this? Talk about being shunted into something she really did not want to do! Still, just a few days, she'd said. What harm could it do? As long as Kirsty didn't get her painted talons into Rob: her good-looking, charming, far too easy-going husband.

Rob. Well hadn't she got that one wrong? She'd been looking in entirely the opposite direction, and by the time she knew for sure that Kirsty was seeing Jamie, it was already way too late. During her time with them, the woman had behaved impeccably. Arriving with a huge bouquet of flowers for Helen and two bottles of red wine for Rob, she had pretty much kept to her room after taking them out for dinner. On Sunday she'd disappeared to her parents' for lunch and by Tuesday she had gone, leaving a box of chocolates and an envelope with a fifty-pound note tucked inside. At the time they'd been pleased.

But Kirsty's work had been done. Executed with all the swiftness of a trained assassin. A flash of kohl rimmed eyes over the dinner table. Red stiletto heels. A transparent dressing gown. And she had Jamie's number.

Helen had been observing Rob. Watching to see if his eyes brightened when Kirsty walked in the room, how attentive he was, if his mood altered when Kirsty left. But it wasn't Rob

All at once Aunt Martha had been quite ruthlessly abandoned – Kirsty no longer swooping down on the nursing home every other day. Then there came Jamie's coy reaction to her question about who he was seeing one evening. Followed by a casual slip of a remark about older women. A sly smile. A furtive mobile phone conversation. Kirsty. She bloody knew it.

Probably, it was around that time the evil thoughts started. They came when least expected and they came with a vengeance - shooting across her brain like poisonous darts. Sometimes they happened just as she was falling asleep, other times she'd be leaning over someone's bed, tucking them in. In a flash would come an image: Kirsty held at gunpoint; Kirsty drowning - face bloated and gasping; or lying broken and bent like a puppet after tripping down a flight of steps; or maybe stuck in a lift that was plummeting to the basement…

And once they started they wouldn't stop. She'd be spooning out fruit salad when whoosh - Kirsty's parachute cord failed. Administering insulin when bam - Kirsty's plane hurtled into the side of a mountain. Sipping tea with bereaved relatives when alas, poor Kirsty choked into her poisonous mushrooms. Like a door that had opened slightly her visions kept coming, slipping through the gap until she could no longer control them, couldn't sleep nights, her head hurt and her eyes burned.

***

So here she is after waiting round the corner from the wine bar in the tomb like stillness of her parked car. Fingers and toes numb, teeth chattering, she has watched Kirsty and Jamie leave the bar together, his arm around her shoulder while she chats on the phone to someone else, shrugging Jamie away.

Last night Jamie told her he was leaving home - moving in with someone and not going to university. He didn't want to do what she wanted him to do - needed to do his own thing. He'd slammed his bedroom door. Started packing. Wouldn't say where or who or why.

No. This could and would not happen, that's all she knew.

That woman was not going to use her son, spit him out and ruin his life. Her foot slams to the floor and the engine screams.

Doing it……now!

A sudden, sharp rap at her window causes her heart to jackhammer against her ribs and the car slams to a halt.

"What the hell do you think you're doing, Woman?" A man is shouting through the steamed up passenger window. "You nearly killed me."

Helen squints up at him. He is on a bike, gesticulating madly. She glances ahead. In time to catch Kirsty wrenching open the door to her car and jumping in. Headlights flood the wet tarmac before she quickly vanishes into the traffic. Helen buzzes down the window. "I'm so sorry. I didn't see you."

The man glares and then relents. "All in one piece. Just remember to use your mirrors next time, okay?"

Helen nods. A horn peeps. Fresh air fills the car. That man on the bike has saved them all. Rob. In her mind she sees Rob's face as it might have been - ashen and drawn – as she faces the dock in court.

With violently shaking hands, she grips the steering wheel and starts the engine up again. Deep breaths. How close she came.

And then a sudden movement in the shadows catches her eye.

She recognises his huddled shape in the bus shelter. Swinging the car round to a blasting of angry horns, Helen pulls alongside him and he climbs in.

They drive for a few minutes in silence before Jamie says, "Not really her night, was it?"

"Pardon?"

"First me dumping her and then you trying to run her over."

Confusion clouds her thoughts. "But, I thought–"

"I didn't dare tell you, Mum. Sorry – but me and Steve want to backpack for a year. She didn't like it either."

"And it's Steve you're moving in with, not..?"

A cold sweat breaks out down Helen's back, washing over her in a shudder. If she ever saw that man on the bike again she'd have to pin him to the ground and kiss him.

The End

Sixty Seconds was first published by: 1. The Weekly News, UK. 2011 and   2. Ether books.com 2012

19. House Hunt

So far it had been a disaster. Josie sat, arms folded, staring at the scenery whizzing past: another petrol station, another row of houses… her interest long gone. Nothing they saw now could possibly pick up her mood.

The day had started badly. The first house, after a long drive to the South coast, had been deserted. No one home. No key. No estate agent. Nothing. Tired and tetchy, Josie and Phil stared at each other in disbelief.

"You must have got the wrong day," Phil said.

Josie scrabbled for her diary, and pointed to the correct date and time quite clearly written after confirming with the agents the day before. She'd wanted to scream, really badly, but by then a kindly neighbour had appeared and she'd had to put on a brave face.

The next house had been a gorgeous old cottage with wisteria clambering up the yellow stone walls. Her spirits had lifted. Momentarily. The ceiling beams were so low Phil could barely straighten up, and the staircase so narrow they'd had to scuttle up like mice. That was when she knew it was going to be one of those days. "This isn't looking good either," she muttered, as Phil turned the car onto a long, straight windswept road.

"Does look a bit bleak,' Phil admitted.

Poor Phil; they'd been house-hunting for weeks now and he was due to start his new job next month. They really did have to find somewhere.

The road began to bend and wind and they saw on the left a small copse and a lichgate.

"Aha!" Phil brightened. "This must be it."

It certainly looked like the photograph on the brochure: a stone church nestling in a cluster of evergreens.

"I like it," he said, as they walked up to the huge oak door. He pulled on the rope and a large iron bell clanged dramatically. "Wow!"

Josie smiled nervously. "Why do I suddenly feel like I'm in a Hitchcock film?" she asked, just as the door swung open.

The church had been converted just a few years previously – and the dining room, photographed to spectacular effect in the brochure, did not disappoint. A long table had been stage set with full dinner service and wine goblets.

"Wow!" said Phil, again.

The owner beamed proudly. "And these," he said, pointing to stones set in the walls, "are memorial tablets. This one's dated 1485. Now, shall I organise some tea while you both have a wander?"

Josie looked through an archway to a dark, windowless cavern where a woman and a young girl were baking cakes. "Lovely. Thank you."

"Come on,' said Phil. "Let's go look

upstairs."

Phil was grinning, Josie noted with some degree of alarm. He loved it. In fact she reckoned he'd already made up his mind But it was she who would be spending time alone here, and for an illustrator the place was dark. She ducked to enter the main bedroom. "I bet it's haunted,' she whispered.

Phil squeezed her hand. "Yeah - great, isn't it?"

Downstairs they found a log fire crackling invitingly, and the woman they'd seen earlier was curled up on the sofa with a child.

"Hi, I'm Ellie," said the woman. "And this is Flora, my daughter."

"Josie. Hi." They shook hands.

"Your husband seems very taken with the place?"

"Yes."

Phil was talking to the man they now knew as Alex, admiring the garden. Or, more accurately - graveyard. *They had to get out of here*. Josie took a welcome sip of hot tea. "Have you had much interest?"

Ellie laughed. "Oh they're all frightened out of their wits. It's the gravestones - not everyone can live in a church."

Josie swallowed another gulp of tea, plucking up courage to ask the next question. She feigned a light, carefree laugh. "Frightened? Er...of ghosts you mean?" Immediately Flora grinned wickedly and looked set to open her mouth when Ellie quickly interjected, "We don't have ghosts," she said firmly. But Josie noticed her grip on Flora's shoulder tighten, and Flora had begun to look agitated, kicking her heels against the sofa.

"I know," Ellie called out to her husband. "Let's show them the garden, Alex." A bank of black cloud, edging closer, was casting a dark shadow over the church, whipping up a sharp breeze. And reluctant to move from the warm fire after a long, tiring day, Josie stayed pinned to her seat. "Actually, I think I'll stay here if you don't mind?"

"Sure. Flora will keep you company."

Good. If there was one thing she knew about kids - they told it like it was.

"So," she said to Flora once they were alone. "How do you feel about having gravestones in the garden? It must be spooky sometimes?"

"They're not harmful, you know," said Flora, with an air of authority. Then more sheepishly, "Granny says we do have ghosts though, and she won't come to stay with us anymore."

"Really?"

"Yes, she said someone was trying to pull the bedclothes off her bed all night."

Eek! "Has that ever happened to you?"

Flora shook her head. "No. Apart from Arthur. But he's a friendly ghost."

"Uh-huh." Yup. They definitely had to get out of here.

The ominous black cloud was now directly overhead and it wasn't long before the others practically blew back in through the French windows, the doors slamming shut behind them.

"Oh, we'll definitely be in touch," Phil said, handing Alex his business card. "We absolutely love it, don't we, darling?"

Josie nodded and smiled. Over her dead body!

"Apart from the fact that it's dark and haunted, it's totally isolated," she argued as they drove away. "Look! Look around you!"

Sure enough, as soon as they turned out of the driveway, the landscape was bleak and barren again. Around them the wind howled.

"Can you see anywhere to turn round?" said Phil, glancing at the time. There was still another house to see.

"How long to get there?"

"About half an hour. Ah, here we go." He swung the car into a narrow lane flanked by swaying trees. And then stopped dead. In front of them was an entire village: a row of stone cottages, a stream, a manor house and a church. "This must be what Alex was talking about," Phil cried excitedly. "He said the whole area was an ancient Saxon settlement. Blimey - look at it."

Josie, with her artist's eye, noticed the eerie, low golden light and the wild, dark sky skirting around it. There wasn't a soul in sight.

But Phil was now in raptures about the fascinating history and buying a metal detector for ancient treasures. Eventually, noticing her silence he glanced over and patted her hand. "You're not seriously spooked are you?"

Josie nodded. "I can't live here." And then

felt rotten because he looked so crestfallen. "Let's just see what the next house is like before we decide, okay?"

"You don't seem to like anything," he grumbled.

That was unfair and he knew it. The move from North to South was a huge task and so far they'd seen cottages Phil couldn't stand up in, and houses either on busy junctions or needing total renovation, when neither of them were any good at DIY. All of which made the church appeal so much to Phil. It had character, he argued. It had space. It had history. Peace and quiet…

Josie bit her lip. Time was running out.

Half an hour later they pulled up outside a perfectly normal brick house on the outskirts of a working village. There was a pub, a post office, and even a tiny village school. Josie smiled. Normality. Why had it been so hard to find?

A pleasant looking lady in her late fifties, opened the door, wiping her hands on her apron. "Madeline Oliver," she said, offering her hand. "Come on in. You must be exhausted travelling all the way from Yorkshire? I'll put the kettle on while you have a look round."

The house was large, light and airy. The garden swept down to a delightful stream and there was even an outhouse that could be used as a studio.

"It's perfect," Josie beamed.

Phil shrugged.

"Oh come on," she urged as they strolled hand in hand around the garden. "I can live here when you're away without being scared to death. There are neighbours, a shop and a community. Even a studio. Look Phil, we're not going to get any better than this and it's a good price too."

Phil looked around and eventually nodded. "Well I liked the church but, well, you do need to feel safe and–"

Josie leaned into him and squeezed his arm.

Ten minutes later they were getting back into the car amid promises of phoning the agent first thing. The light was fading fast and they had a long journey home but finally, finally - the search was over.

***

Madeline Oliver watched as their taillights disappeared round the corner, then glanced at her watch. She mustn't be late. Tonight was a full moon, and as High Priestess of the coven she must set up the altar before tonight's ceremony. The whole village would be there. And there was news - they had newcomers to look forward to welcoming soon. Very soon.

THE END

House Hunt was first published by My Weekly, UK. 2008

20. The Witchfinders

Beth pulled her cloak tightly around her. The last day of October and the air was damp and chill, the death of Autumn leaves lying ankle deep in the woods, smoke curling into the night air from her distant cottage. Not far to go now. She bent her head, fear knotting her stomach, knowing what she had yet to pass on the lane.

The party in town had turned riotous. What had at first been ghoulish fancy dress, cut-out gourds and innocent apple-bobbing, had quickly escalated into fighting when the witch finders arrived. 1645 was a dangerous year for young girls not married, and two selling corn dollies had just been dragged away from the market place. Reputedly, and from a reliable source, said the witch finders, they had the devil's marks on them. One had a mole on her neck and the other had been seen conversing with a 'familiar' - a large black dog - in the fields near her cottage. The crowd had gasped, closing in around the girls as they were led away screaming their innocence.

Who would tell such tales about young girls to the merciless witch finders? They surely knew the fate that would await them? Scores of young women in these Eastern counties had been burned to death in less than a year. If you didn't bleed you were a witch, they said. If you had renounced baptism then the water would reject you and a witch would float. If you hadn't then you would drown.

Amid the masks and the smoke, witches costumes and beer-swilling, Beth made a quiet escape, leaving her father and brother behind with the pony and trap. *Not far to go. Not far to go.* Breathlessly she emerged from the short cut through the woods and onto the lane that led to the family home. Just the spooky scarecrow to pass. The one that stood alone in the long-since harvested fields with its leery grin and gangly, flapping limbs. Why couldn't their farming neighbours take it down? Instead they left it there for screeching crows to perch on, in their ragged coats of black cloth. And that monster's head to twist and turn as she hurried past.

She broke into a run. *Don't look at it. Don't look at it. It isn't alive - it's just straw and old clothes...*

The October mist had settled on the lowlands like a blanket of soft grey down, thickening the night air. It was hard to see more than a few footsteps ahead and the light from her lantern glowed a woolly yellow. She kept her eyes firmly on the cottage lights ahead, stumbling on determinedly towards the glow of a fire in the downstairs room, and a lamp left burning in her bedroom window.

After all, it was Halloween and only fools left themselves and their homes unprotected. By midnight Samhain would begin - two days during which the lining between the living and the dead overlapped and the dead came to life. The only way to protect yourself was to wear masks and costumes, light bonfires and hang lanterns. Confusion was all. By midnight a young girl must be home. It was a huge relief to push open the cottage door, and bolt it behind her. *Something about that scarecrow...*

Her father said she was being ridiculous - that her imagination was wildly out of control. He'd painstakingly shown her how to make her own scarecrow for their small vegetable plot. And yet...there was just something about that one on the lane.... It haunted her, of course, haunting her dreams as she dozed in front of the fire while the cat purred contentedly on her lap – its arms of straw scratching at the windows, slashed-out eyes peering in.

Someone was there!

She woke with a start, suddenly fully, overly, alert. And the cat was meowing - prowling restlessly back and forth across the window ledge. Something, or someone, was definitely outside – that was no dream!

She strained her ears. Dull, scraping footsteps. Coming nearer. It was almost midnight. The scarecrow - of course - the scarecrow had come to life just like she always knew it would.

Beth's heart banged hard against her ribs as with shaking hands she picked up her father's heavy musket. Midnight chimed. Samhain had begun. Her poor father and brother would be coming home, dull witted with drink, relying on the old pony to trot along the familiar route. The monster would surely kill them.

Trembling, she leaned against the barred door, listening to heavy, wheezy breathing that sounded like an old man with a bad chest - getting louder - footsteps dragging in the ground as if one leg was dead; a smell of wet straw and rotting leaves. She waited, expecting the lightest of taps, or a toothless dead-eyed face staring through the window.

Instead the door was suddenly pounded with iron fists making it rattle on its hinges, and she flew backwards. That bolt, she knew, would not hold for long. Over and over the unseen force behind the door, pummelled and kicked until finally and inevitably, the door splintered. There was now no choice but to lift the heavy musket and fire. *Be gone horrible scarecrow. Be gone!*

In the silent seconds that followed Beth picked up her lantern and found, to her amazement, not a scarecrow lying on the ground but two grown men. The witchfinders! Sent, she quickly realised, to arrest her - a thirteen year old girl. One of the men groaned, clearly still alive. She reached for the iron kettle, fire hot, and swung it clean against his skull.

To think that all this time she'd been frightened of a stupid scarecrow, firing blindly at what she thought was a bundle of sticks come to life! Like her old dad always said – the only thing you need be frightened of is flesh and blood.

But who had sent them out here? It seemed there were people in this town who had called in the witch finders deliberately, and chosen for her a sure death. How could they do that? Well they had better start praying because she would hunt them down and she would make them pay.

***

From the fields opposite the scarecrow swayed and drooped from its post in the darkness. The young girl in the cottage had her hands raised and her face held up to the night sky as she chanted her vengeance.

A few stars glittered between the parting clouds. Samhain. A time for the dead to rise, although he was sorely weakened in his guise as a scarecrow. He'd done what he had to, to warn her they were coming - put her on her guard, scratching at her door and windows to wake her. A girl with a cat. A girl who cast magic circles, stuck pins in effigies and made herbal potions. A witch who would now wreak revenge.

Good, he thought with a dry chuckle. Confusion reigned - let Halloween commence.

THE END

The Witchfinders was first published by: 1. The Weekly News, 27/10/2011, 2. That's Life Fast Fiction, Australia, 2012

***

Father of Lies
A Darkly Disturbing Occult Horror Trilogy: Book 1

Boy did this pack a punch and scare me witless..'
'Scary as hell...What I thought would be mainstream horror was anything but...'
'Not for the faint-hearted. Be warned - this is very, very dark subject matter.'
'A truly wonderful and scary start to a horror trilogy. One of the best and most well written books I've read in a long time.'
'A dark and compelling read. I devoured it in one afternoon. Even as the horrors unfolded I couldn't race through the pages quickly enough for more...'
'Delivers the spooky in spades!'
'Will go so far as to say Sarah is now my favourite author - sorry Mr King!'

'Ruby is the most violently disturbed patient ever admitted to Drummersgate Asylum, high on the bleak moors of northern England. With no improvement after two years, Dr. Jack McGowan finally decides to take a risk and hypnotises her. With terrifying consequences.
A horrific dark force is now unleashed on the entire medical team, as each in turn attempts to unlock Ruby's shocking and sinister past. Who is this girl? And how did she manage to survive such

unimaginable evil? Set in a desolate ex-mining village, where secrets are tightly kept and intruders hounded out, their questions soon lead to a haunted mill, the heart of darkness...and The Father of Lies.'

***

Tanners Dell – Book 2

Now only one of the original team remains – Ward Sister, Becky. However, despite her fiancé, Callum, being unconscious and many of her colleagues either dead or critically ill, she is determined to rescue Ruby's twelve year old daughter from a similar fate to her mother.
But no one asking questions in the desolate ex-mining village Ruby hails from ever comes to a good end. And as the diabolical history of the area is gradually revealed, it seems the evil invoked is both real and contagious.
Don't turn the lights out yet!

***

Magda – Book 3

The dark and twisted community of Woodsend harbours a terrible secret – one tracing back to the age of the Elizabethan witch hunts, when many innocent women were persecuted and hanged. But there is a far deeper vein of horror running through this village; an evil that once invoked has no intention of relinquishing its grip on the modern world. Rather it watches and waits with focused intelligence, leaving Ward Sister, Becky, and CID Officer, Toby, constantly checking over their shoulders and jumping at shadows.

Just who invited in this malevolent presence? And is the demonic woman who possessed Magda back in the sixteenth century, the same one now gazing at Becky whenever she looks in the mirror?

Are you ready to meet Magda in this final instalment of the trilogy? Are you sure?

***

Out April 26th, 2018

The Owlmen
Pure Occult Horror
If They See You They Will Come For You

Ellie Blake is recovering from a nervous breakdown. Deciding to move back to her northern roots, she and her psychiatrist husband buy Tanners Dell at auction - an old water mill in the moorland village of Bridesmoor.

However, there is disquiet in the village. Tanners Dell has a terrible secret, one so well guarded no one speaks its name. But in her search for meaning and very much alone, Ellie is drawn to traditional witchcraft and determined to pursue it. All her life she has been cowed. All her life she has apologised for her very existence. And witchcraft has opened a door she could never have imagined. Imbued with power and overawed with its magick, for the first time she feels she has come home, truly knows who she is.

Tanners Dell though, with its centuries old demonic history...well, it's a dangerous place for a novice...

http://www.amazon.co.uk/dp/B079W9FKV7
http://www.amazon.com/dp/B079W9FKV7

***

The Soprano – A Haunting Supernatural Thriller

It is 1951 and a remote mining village on the North Staffordshire Moors is hit by one of the worst snowstorms in living memory. Cut off for over three weeks, the old and the sick will die; the strongest bunker down; and those with evil intent will bring to its conclusion a family vendetta spanning three generations.
Inspired by a true event, 'The Soprano' tells the story of Grace Holland - a strikingly beautiful, much admired local celebrity who brings glamour and inspiration to the grimy moorland community. But why is Grace still here? Why doesn't she leave this staunchly Methodist, rain-sodden place and the isolated farmhouse she shares with her mother? Riddled with witchcraft and tales of superstition, the story is mostly narrated by the Whistler family who own the local funeral parlour, in particular six year old Louise - now an elderly lady - who recalls one of the most shocking crimes imaginable.
http://www.amazon.co.uk/dp/B0737GQ9Qhttp://www.amazon.com/dp/B0737GQ9Q7

***

If you enjoy supernatural horror and dark psychological thrillers, why not visit Sarah England's website. There is an infrequent newsletter sign-up available too.
www.sarahenglandauthorauthor.co.uk